Dream Story

Arthur Schnitzler

Dream Story

Translated by
J. M. Q. Davies

PENGUIN CLASSICS
an imprint of
PENGUIN BOOKS

PENGUIN CLASSICS

UK | USA | Canada | Ireland | Australia
India | New Zealand | South Africa

Penguin Books is part of the Penguin Random House group of companies
whose addresses can be found at global.penguinrandomhouse.com.

Penguin
Random House
UK

First published in German as *Traumnovelle* 1926
First published in Penguin Classics 1999
This edition published in Little Clothbound Classics 2023
002

Cover design and illustration by Coralie Bickford-Smith

Translation copyright © J. M. Q. Davies, 1999

Set in 10/14.5pt Baskerville 10 Pro
Typeset by Jouve (UK), Milton Keynes
Printed and bound in Great Britain by Clays Ltd, Elcograf S.p.A.

The authorized representative in the EEA is Penguin Random House Ireland,
Morrison Chambers, 32 Nassau Street, Dublin D02 YH68

A CIP catalogue record for this book is available from the British Library

ISBN: 978-0-241-62022-9

Dream Story

I

'Twenty-four brown slaves rowed the splendid galley that would bring Prince Amgiad to the Caliph's palace. But the Prince, wrapped in his purple cloak, lay alone on the deck beneath the deep blue, star-spangled night sky, and his gaze –'

Up to this point the little girl had been reading aloud; now, quite suddenly, her eyes closed. Her parents looked at each other with a smile, and Fridolin bent over her, kissed her flaxen hair, and snapped shut the book that was resting on the table, which had not as yet been cleared. The child looked up as if caught out.

'Nine o'clock,' said her father, 'time for bed.' And as Albertine too had now bent over the child, the parents' hands touched as they fondly stroked her brow, and, with a tender smile that was no longer intended solely for the child, their eyes met. The maid came in and bade the little one say goodnight to her parents; obediently she got up, proffered her lips to her father and mother to be kissed, and let the maid escort her quietly from the room. Left alone under the reddish glow of the hanging lamp, Fridolin and Albertine suddenly felt impelled to resume the discussion of their experiences at yesterday's masked ball, which they had begun before the evening meal.

It had been their first ball of the year, which they had decided to attend just before the close of the Carnival season. Immediately upon entering the ballroom, Fridolin had been greeted like an impatiently awaited friend by two dominoes dressed in red, whom he had not managed to identify, even though they were remarkably well informed about various episodes from his hospital and student days. They had left the box to which they had invited him with such auspicious friendliness, promising to return shortly unmasked, but then had stayed away so long that he became impatient and decided to descend to the ground floor, hoping to meet the two enigmatic creatures there again. He looked around intently, without, however, catching sight of them; instead, quite unexpectedly, another female reveller took him by the arm: it was his wife. She had just withdrawn rather abruptly from a stranger, whose blasé, melancholy air and foreign-sounding – evidently Polish – accent had at first intrigued her, but who had then suddenly let slip a surprisingly crude and insolent remark that had hurt and even frightened her. And so man and wife, glad at heart to have escaped a disappointingly banal charade, were soon sitting in the refreshment room over oysters and champagne, like two lovers among other amorous couples, and chatting amiably drew one another, as if they had just become acquainted, into a game of gallantry, seduction, resistance and fulfilment; and then, after a swift coach-ride through the white winter's night, they sank into one another's arms with an ardour they had not experienced for quite some time. A grey morning awoke them all too soon. The husband's profession summoned him to his patients' bedsides at an early hour, and the duties of housekeeper and mother did not allow Albertine to rest much longer. And so the time had passed predictably and soberly enough in work and routine chores, and the events of the previous night from first to last had faded; and only now that both their days' work was over, the child asleep and no further disturbance anticipated, did the shadowy figures from the masked ball, the melancholy stranger and the dominoes in red, revive; and those trivial encounters became magically and painfully inter-fused with the treacherous illusion of missed opportunities. Innocent yet ominous questions and vague ambiguous answers passed to and fro between them; and, as neither of them doubted the other's absolute candour, both felt the need for mild revenge. They exaggerated the extent to which their masked partners had attracted them, made fun of the jealous stirrings the other revealed, and lied dismissively about their own. Yet this light banter about the trivial adventures of the previous night led to more serious discussion of those hidden, scarcely admitted desires which are apt to raise dark and perilous storms even in the purest, most transparent soul; and they talked about those secret regions for which they felt hardly any longing, yet towards which the irrational winds of fate might one day drive them, if only in their dreams. For however much they might belong to one another heart and soul, they knew last night was not the first time they had been stirred by a whiff of free-dom, danger and adventure. With self-tormenting anxiety and sordid curiosity, each sought to coax admissions from the other; while drawing closer in their fear, each groped for any fact, however slight, any experience, however trivial, which might articulate the fundamentally inexpressible confession of a truth capable of releasing them from the tension and mistrust that were slowly starting to become intolerable. Whether it was because she was the more impetuous, the more honest or the more warmhearted, Albertine was the first to find the courage to make a frank confession; and with a trembling voice she asked Fridolin if he remembered a young man the previous summer on the Danish coast who had been sitting with two officers at the table next to them one evening, and who, on receiving a telegram during the meal, had promptly taken a hasty leave of his two friends.

Fridolin nodded. 'What about him?' he asked.

'That same morning I'd seen him once before,' replied Albertine, 'as he was hurrying up the hotel stairs with his yellow suitcase. He'd glanced at me as we passed, but a few steps further up he stopped and turned round towards me – our eyes couldn't help meeting. He didn't smile, indeed his face seemed to cloud over, and I must have reacted likewise, because I felt moved as never before. The whole day I lay on the beach, lost in dreams. Were he to summon me – or so I believed – I wouldn't have been able to resist. I thought myself capable of doing anything; I felt I had as good as resolved to relinquish you, the child, my future, yet at the same time – will you believe this? – you were more dear to me than ever. It was that same afternoon, you remember, that we spoke so confidingly about a thousand things, discussing our future together, talking about the child as we hadn't done for ages. Then at sunset, when we were sitting on the balcony, he walked past us on the beach below without looking up, and I was overjoyed to see him. But it was you whose brow I stroked and hair I kissed, and in my love for you there was also a good deal of distressing pity. That evening I wore a white rose in my belt, and you yourself said that I looked very beautiful. Perhaps it was no coincidence that the stranger was sitting near us with his friends. He didn't look across at me, but I toyed with the idea of stepping over to his table and saying to him, "Here I am, my long-awaited one, my beloved – take me away." At that moment they brought him the telegram: he read it, went pale, whispered a few words to the younger of the two officers, and with an enigmatic look in my direction left the room.'

'And then?' asked Fridolin drily, as she fell silent.

'Nothing more. All I know is that next morning I awoke feeling nervous and distressed. What I was anxious about – whether it was that he had left, or that he might still be there – I don't know, and even then I didn't know. Yet when at noon he still hadn't appeared, I heaved a sigh of relief. Don't question me further, Fridolin, I've told you the whole truth. – You too had some sort of experience on that beach – of that I'm certain.'

Fridolin got up, paced up and down the room a few times, then said, 'You're right.' He stood at the window, his face in darkness. 'In the morning,' he began in a restrained, somewhat resentful tone, 'often very early before you got up, I would wander along the shore out past the resort; yet, early as it was, the sun would always be shining brightly over the sea. Out there along the shore, as you know, there were little houses, each a small world unto its own, some with fenced-off gardens, some just surrounded by woods, and the bathing-huts were separated from the

Arthur Schnitzler

houses by the road and by a stretch of sand. I seldom encountered anybody, and there were never any bathers at that hour. One morning, however, I suddenly became aware of a female figure, not visible before, who was gingerly advancing along the narrow gangplank of one of those bathing-huts on stilts, putting one foot in front of the other and stretching her arms behind as she groped along the wooden wall. She was a young girl of no more than fifteen, her loose, blonde hair falling over her shoulders and on one side across her tender breast. Gazing down into the water, she slowly inched her way with lowered eyes along the wall towards the near corner of the hut, and suddenly emerged directly opposite where I was standing; she reached behind her even further with her arms, as if to gain a firmer hold, looked up and suddenly caught sight of me. Her whole body began to tremble, as though she were about to either fall or to run away. But, as she could only have proceeded very slowly along the narrow plank, she decided not to move – and so she just stood there, looking at first frightened, then angry and finally embarrassed. But all at once she smiled, a ravishing smile; indeed there was a welcoming twinkle in her eye – and at the same time a

gentle mockery about the way she lightly skimmed
the water between us with her foot. Then she stretched
her young, slender body, as though exulting in her
beauty, and evidently proud and sweetly aroused at
feeling my ardent gaze upon her. We stood opposite
each other like this for perhaps ten seconds, with lips
half open and eyes aflame. Involuntarily I stretched
out my arms towards her: there was joy and abandon
in her gaze. But all at once she shook her head vigorously, let go of the side of the hut with one hand, and
peremptorily signalled that I should withdraw; and,
when I could not bring myself to obey at once, such
a pleading, such a beseeching look came into her
child's eyes that I had no alternative but to turn away.
I hastily resumed my walk without once turning
round – not out of consideration, obedience or chiv-
alry, but because I'd felt so profoundly moved by her
parting look, far transcending anything I'd experienced before, that I was on the point of swooning.'
And with that he ended.

'And how often,' asked Albertine flatly, looking
straight ahead, 'did you later follow the same path?'

'All I've told you,' replied Fridolin, 'just happened
to occur on the last day of our stay in Denmark. Even

I don't know how things might have developed under other circumstances. And you too, Albertine, shouldn't inquire any further.'

He was still standing at the window, motionless. Albertine got up and went over to him, her eyes dark and moist, her brow slightly creased. 'In future we should always tell each other things like this at once,' she said.

He nodded silently.

'Promise me.'

He drew her to him. 'Do you really doubt that?' he asked; but his voice still sounded harsh.

She took his hands, fondled them and looked up at him with tearful eyes, in the depths of which he tried to read her thoughts. She was now thinking about the other, more real experiences of his youth, some of which she was privy to, since during the first years of their marriage he had given way to her jealous curiosity rather too eagerly and revealed, or, as it often seemed to him, surrendered many things he should perhaps have kept to himself. He could tell that various memories were now resurfacing within her with some urgency, and so he was hardly surprised when, as if in a dream, she mentioned the half-forgotten name of one of his youthful loves. Yet to him it came across as a reproach, even as a quiet threat.

He drew her hands to his lips.

'In every woman – believe me, even though it may sound trite – in every woman with whom I thought I was in love, it was always you that I was searching for. I feel this more deeply, Albertine, than you can ever understand.'

She smiled sadly. 'And what if I too had chosen to go exploring first?' she said. Her expression changed, becoming inscrutable and cold. He let go her hands, as if he had caught her out in a lie or infidelity; but she continued, 'Ah, if only you all knew,' and again fell silent.

'If we only knew – What do you mean by that?'

Rather harshly she replied, 'More or less, my dear, what you imagine.'

'Albertine – is there something you've never told me?'

She nodded with a strange smile and looked straight ahead. Vague, irrational doubts began to stir within him.

'I don't quite understand,' he said. 'You were scarcely seventeen when we became engaged.'

'Yes, Fridolin, a little over sixteen. And yet' – she looked him straight in the eye – 'it was not my fault if I was still a virgin when I became your wife.'

'Albertine!'

And she continued, 'It was on the Wörthersee, shortly before our engagement, Fridolin, when one beautiful summer evening an extremely handsome youth appeared outside my window, which looked out over broad extensive meadows. We chatted away together, and in the course of our conversation I thought to myself, just listen to what I thought: what a sweet delightful young person he is – he would only have to say the word this minute, though of course it would have to be the right one, and I would go out and join him in the meadows and follow him wherever he desired, into the wood, perhaps; or it would be lovelier still if we were to go out on to the lake together in a boat – and that night he could have everything he desired of me. Yes, that's what I thought to myself. – But he didn't say the word, this charming youth; he just fondly kissed my hand, and the next morning asked me whether I would be his wife. And I said yes.'

Fridolin let her hand go, displeased. 'And what if

that evening,' he remarked, 'someone else had happened to stand outside your window, and had said the right word: for example –' He wondered whose name he should mention, but she stretched out her arm in a gesture of protest.

'Anyone else, whoever it might have been, could have said what he liked, it would have been to little avail. And if you hadn't been the one to stand before my window,' she said, smiling up at him, 'then the summer evening wouldn't have been so lovely either.'

His mouth twisted in a sneer. 'That's what you say now, so at this moment you may even believe it. But –'

There was a knock at the door. The chambermaid entered and announced that the porter's wife from the Schreyvogelgasse had come to fetch the doctor on behalf of the Court Counsellor, who was again feeling very ill. Fridolin went into the hall, learned from the messenger that the Court Counsellor had had another heart-attack and was in a bad way, and promised to come at once.

'Are you going out?' Albertine asked him as he was hastily preparing to leave, and from her irritable tone it seemed as though he were deliberately treating her unjustly.

A little incredulously, Fridolin answered, 'But I have to.'

She sighed lightly.

'It shouldn't be too bad, I hope,' said Fridolin, 'in the past, three grams of morphine have usually helped him over the attack.'

The chambermaid brought his fur coat. Fridolin kissed Albertine on the mouth and forehead a little absent-mindedly, as if the last hour's conversation had already been erased from his memory, and hurried off.

Out on the street he had to unbutton his fur coat. There had been a sudden thaw, the snow on the pavements had almost completely melted, and there was a breath of the coming spring in the air. From Fridolin's apartment near the General Hospital in the Josefstadt it was barely a quarter of an hour's walk to the Schreyvogelgasse; and so Fridolin soon found himself climbing the ill-lit, winding stairs of the old house to the second floor and tugging at the bell; but, even before the old-fashioned tinkling resounded, he noticed that the door was ajar; he stepped through the unlit hall into the living-room and realized immediately that he had arrived too late. The green-shaded kerosene lamp hanging from the ceiling cast a dim light over the bed-cover, under which an emaciated body was stretched out motionless. The dead man's face was in shadow, but Fridolin knew it so well that he imagined he could see it quite distinctly – gaunt, wrinkled, the high forehead, the full short white beard, the strikingly ugly ears with their white hairs. The Court Counsellor's daughter, Marianne, sat at the foot of the bed, her arms hanging limply by her sides as if in utter exhaustion. There was a smell of old furniture, medicaments, kerosene, the kitchen; also a whiff of eau de Cologne and rose-water, and somehow Fridolin could even sense the stale sweetish smell of this pale girl, who though still young had for months, for years, been losing her bloom in the course of heavy household chores, tiring care and nocturnal vigils.

When Fridolin entered, she turned to look at him, but in the meagre light he had difficulty making out whether her cheeks turned red as they usually did when he appeared. She was on the point of getting up, but a gesture from Fridolin prevented her, and, nodding, she greeted him with her large, sorrowful eyes. He approached the head of the bed, mechanically felt the dead man's temples, then the wrists that protruded from the wide, open sleeves resting on the bed-cover, then shrugged his shoulders in a mild gesture of regret and put his hands in the pockets of his fur coat, his gaze wandering round the room and eventually coming to rest on Marianne. Her hair was thick and fair but dry, her neck well formed and slender but of a yellowish complexion and no longer completely free of wrinkles, and her lips pinched as if from many unspoken words.

'Well now, my dear young lady,' he said softly and almost in embarrassment, 'you were scarcely unprepared for it.'

She stretched out her hand towards him. He took it sympathetically, asking dutifully about the last fatal attack, whereupon she related everything factually and briefly, and then described the last relatively tranquil days during which Fridolin had not seen the sick man. Fridolin drew up a chair, seating himself opposite Marianne, and to console her intimated that in his last hour her father would hardly have suffered at all; then he asked if the relatives had been informed. Yes, the porter's wife was already on the way to her uncle, and in any case Dr Roediger would soon be there. 'My fiancé,' she added, glancing at Fridolin's forehead rather than looking him in the eye.

Fridolin merely nodded. In the course of a year he had met Dr Roediger two or three times here in the house. This pale, excessively slim young man with glasses and a short blond beard, a lecturer in history at Vienna University, had made a favourable impression on him, without, however, rousing any further curiosity. Marianne would certainly look better than she did, he thought, if she were his mistress. Her hair would be less dry, her lips redder and fuller. How old would she be? he wondered. When I was first called out to the Court Counsellor's three or four years ago, she was twenty-three. Her mother was still alive then. She was more cheerful when her mother was alive. Didn't she take singing lessons for a while? So she's going to marry this lecturer. Why is she doing it? Certainly she isn't in love with him and he can't have much money either. What sort of marriage will it turn out to be? Well, a marriage like a thousand others. What concern is it of mine? It's quite possible that I shall never see her again, since I will no longer have any function in this house. Ah, how many people I've never seen again, who were closer to me than she is.

While these thoughts were running through his head, Marianne had begun to talk about the dead man, moreover with a certain urgency, as though by virtue of the mere fact of his death he had suddenly become a person of distinction. Was he really only fifty-four years old? Of course, the many worries and disappointments, his wife forever ailing, and his son too had given him a great deal of trouble! What, she had a brother? Yes, certainly! Surely she had told the doctor about him once before. The brother was now living abroad somewhere, and hanging in Marianne's bedroom was a picture he had painted at fifteen. It showed an officer galloping down a hill. Her father had always pretended not to notice this painting. But it was a good painting. Her brother might have gone a long way under more favourable circumstances.

How excitedly she talks, thought Fridolin, and how her eyes are sparkling. Fever perhaps? Quite possibly. She's grown thinner recently. Probably acute bronchitis.

She talked on and on, but to him it seemed as if she didn't really know whom she was talking to, or as if she were talking to herself. For twelve years now her brother had been away from home, indeed she had still been a child when he had suddenly disappeared. It would be four years ago at Christmas since they had last received news of him from some small Italian town. Strange, she had forgotten its name.

She continued talking thus a while aimlessly and almost without logical connection about indifferent matters, then suddenly stopped and sat there silently, her head in her hands. Fridolin was tired and even more bored, and waited anxiously for the relatives or the fiancé to arrive. The silence in the room became oppressive. He felt as though the dead man were joining in their silence, not because he could no longer talk, but deliberately and out of sheer malice.

And with a sidelong glance at him Fridolin said, 'At least as things stand, Marianne, you won't have to remain in this apartment much longer.' And as she raised her head a little, yet without looking up at Fridolin, he continued, 'No doubt your fiancé will soon be offered a professorship; the situation in the humanities is in that respect much more promising than with us.' He reflected that years ago he too had aspired to an academic career, but that with his preference for a comfortable existence he had in the end decided to pursue the more practical side of his profession; and suddenly he saw himself in relation to the excellent Dr Roediger as the lesser man.

'We'll be moving in the autumn,' said Marianne

without stirring, 'he's received an offer from Göttingen.'

'Ah,' said Fridolin, and wanted to congratulate her in some way, but this hardly seemed the appropriate moment. He glanced at the closed window and, as if exercising his prerogative as a physician, opened both wings without asking her permission and let in the breeze, which, having by now become even warmer and more springlike, seemed to bring with it a mild fragrance from the distant wakening woods. When he turned back towards the room, he saw Marianne's eyes turned on him questioningly. He moved closer to her and remarked, 'The fresh air will do you good, I hope. It's become quite warm, and last night—' He was gong to say: we drove home from the masked ball in a flurry of snow, but he hastily reformulated his sentence and concluded, 'Last night the snow in the streets was still half a metre deep.'

She hardly heard what he was saying. Her eyes grew moist, large tears rolled down her cheeks and again she buried her face in her hands. Involuntarily he stretched out his hand and stroked her forehead. He felt her whole body tremble as she began to sob, almost inaudibly at first, then gradually louder and finally without restraint. Suddenly she slipped out of the armchair, prostrated herself at his feet, flung her arms around his knees and pressed her face against them. Then she looked up at him with wide open, wild, agonized eyes and whispered fervently, 'I don't want to leave here. Even if you never came again, and I were never to see you any more, I would still want to live close by you.'

He was more moved than astonished; for he had always known that she was in love with him, or imagined that she was.

'Please get up, Marianne,' he said softly, as he bent down and gently raised her, at the same time thinking: there's a touch of hysteria involved here too, of course. He gave a sidelong glance at her dead father. Suppose he can hear everything, he thought. Suppose he's in a cataleptic trance. Perhaps everyone is only seemingly dead for those first few hours after passing on . . . He held Marianne in his arms but a little apart, and feeling a bit ridiculous he reluctantly pressed a kiss upon her forehead. Fleetingly he recalled a novel he had once read, in which a very young man, almost a boy, had been seduced, or rather raped, at his mother's deathbed by her best friend.

In the same instant, he could not for some reason help thinking of his wife. Bitterness against her welled up inside him, and a sullen resentment of the man with the yellow suitcase on the hotel stairs in Denmark. He drew Marianne closer to him, but without feeling in the least aroused; indeed the sight of her lustreless dry hair and the sweetish-stale smell of her unaired clothes filled him with a faint revulsion. Then the bell rang and, with a sense of being released, he hastily kissed Marianne's hand, as if in gratitude, and went to open the door. Dr Roediger was standing outside in a dark grey overcoat and galoshes, with an umbrella in his hand and an earnest expression befitting the occasion on his face. The two gentlemen nodded to one another with greater familiarity than was warranted by their actual relationship. Then they entered the room together, and Roediger, with an awkward glance at the dead man, extended his sympathies to Marianne. Fridolin went into the next room to see to the death certificate, and, as he turned up the gas flame above the desk, his gaze fell on the picture of an officer in white uniform, charging with sabre drawn down a hill towards an unseen enemy. It was mounted in a narrow gilt frame and the effect was no more impressive than that of a modest lithograph.

Fridolin returned with the completed death certificate to the room where the bridal couple were sitting at the father's bedside, holding hands.

Again the doorbell rang; Roediger got up and went to open it; meanwhile Marianne, her eyes on the floor, said almost inaudibly, 'I love you.' Fridolin's only response was to murmur Marianne's name, not without tenderness. Roediger returned with an older married couple. It was Marianne's uncle and aunt; a few appropriate words were exchanged with the usual awkwardness that the presence of someone recently deceased tends to generate. The little room suddenly seemed to be full of mourning guests, and, feeling himself no longer needed, Fridolin paid his respects. He was conducted to the door by Roediger, who felt obliged to say a few words of thanks and to express the hope that they might meet again before too long.

III

Outside the door to the apartment block, Fridolin looked up at the window he himself had opened earlier; the frames were quivering slightly in the wind that gave a foretaste of spring. The people who had remained behind up there, the living no less than the dead, appeared equally ghostly and unreal to him. It seemed as if he had escaped, not so much from an experience as from some melancholy enchantment that must not gain power over him. The only after-effect he felt was a remarkable reluctance to go home. The snow in the streets had melted, here and there little piles of dirty white snow had accumulated, the gas flames in the streetlamps flickered, and a neigh-bouring church clock struck eleven. Fridolin decided to spend another half-hour in a quiet corner of a coffee-house near his apartment before going to bed and took the route through the Rathauspark. On shadowy benches here and there couples huddled close to one another, as if spring really had arrived and the treacherous warm air were not pregnant with dangers. Stretched out full length on one of the benches lay a ragged-looking man, his hat pressed down over his brow. What if I were to wake him, thought Fridolin, and give him money for a night's lodging? But what good would that do, he went on to reflect, I'd then have to provide for him tomorrow too, otherwise there would be no point, and perhaps I would be suspected of some criminal association with him. And so he quickened his pace, as if to escape all forms of responsibility and temptation as fast as possible. Why him specifically? he asked himself, in Vienna alone there are thousands of such miserable souls. Supposing one were to start worrying about all of them – about the fates of all those unknown people! The dead man he had just left came into his mind, and with a shudder of revulsion he reflected how, in compliance with eternal laws, corruption and decay had already set to work in that emaciated body stretched out full length under the brown flannel coverlet. He was glad that he was still alive, that for him such ugly matters were still probably a long way off; glad that he was in his prime, that a charming and lovable woman was there at his disposal, and that he could have another one, many others, if he so desired. Such things might admittedly require more courage than he could muster; and he reflected that by eight o'clock tomorrow he would be back at the clinic, that he would have to visit his private patients from eleven to one, and hold a seminar from three to five in the afternoon, and that in the evening too he would be faced with a few further house-calls. – Well, with luck at least he would not be summoned in the middle of the night again, as had happened today.

He crossed the Rathausplatz, which glistened faintly like a brownish pond, and turned towards home in the Josefstadt district. In the distance he could hear the regular muffled sound of marching, and still some way off, just rounding a street corner, he saw a small troop of some half dozen fraternity students coming towards him. As the youths emerged into the light of a street lamp, he recognized that they were Alemannians from the blue colours they were sporting. He himself had never belonged to a fraternity, but he had taken part in a few fencing-matches in his time. And the memory of his student days put him in mind of the dominoes in red, who had enticed him into their box the night before and contemptuously abandoned him again so soon. The students were now quite close and were laughing and talking loudly; did he know any of them from the hospital? But in the uncertain light it was impossible to make out their features clearly. He was obliged to stay very close to the wall to avoid colliding with them; now they were past; but the last one to pass him, a lanky fellow in an open winter overcoat and with a bandage over his left eye, seemed quite deliberately to hold back a little and, thrusting his elbow sideways, bumped against him. It could not have been an accident. What does the fellow think he's doing, thought Fridolin, and immediately stopped short; after a couple of steps the student did the same, and so for a moment they eyed one another at close range.

But then Fridolin suddenly turned round again and continued on his way. He heard a short laugh behind him, and was on the point of turning back again to challenge the fellow, but felt his heart beating wildly – exactly as it had about twelve years ago when there had been a loud knocking at his door while he had been entertaining a charming young lady given to rambling on about a – probably non-existent – bridegroom living some way away; though as it turned out it had only been the postman who had been knocking in so threatening a manner. And now he again felt his heart racing, exactly as on that occasion. What's all this, he said to himself peevishly, noticing that his knees were trembling a little. Cowardice? Nonsense! Am I, a man of thirty-five, a practising physician, married and father of a child, really expected to go challenging some drunken student! Challenges! Witnesses! A duel! And perhaps an arm wound into the bargain, all because of a stupid incident like that. And then be professionally incapacitated for a few weeks? Or lose an eye? Or even blood-poisoning? Within a week he could well be as far gone as the gentleman under the brown flannel bed-cover in the Schreyvogelgasse! Cowardice? He had fought in three student fencing-matches, and once had even been prepared to duel with pistols, and it certainly was not on *his* initiative that the matter had then been amicably settled. And what about his profession! Dangers on all sides and at every moment – it was just that one tended to forget about

them. How long ago was it that that child with diphtheria had coughed in his face? No more than three
or four days. Now that was a far more serious matter
than some footling sword-play, and he had not
thought twice about it. Well, if he met the fellow
again, the matter could yet be resolved. He was
scarcely obliged, at midnight on the way to or from
a patient – and after all that might have been the
case – to respond to the absurd effrontery of some
student. Now if on the other hand he were to come
across the young Dane, with whom Albertine – no,
no, what was he thinking of? But then – it really was
no different to her having been his mistress. Worse
even. If only *he* were to come towards him now. What
a pleasure it would be to stand opposite him in some
forest clearing and aim the barrel of his pistol at that
forehead with the fair hair combed across it.

Suddenly he found himself well beyond his
intended destination, in a narrow street where only
a few wretched whores were strolling on their nightly
man-hunt. Like ghosts, he thought. And in his memory the students too, with their blue caps, suddenly
seemed ghost-like, as did Marianne with her fiancé,
uncle and aunt, whom he now imagined sitting hand

in hand around the old Court Counsellor's deathbed; Albertine too, who floated before his mind's eye as she might appear when in deep sleep, her arms tucked beneath her neck, even his child, who lay curled up in her narrow white brass bed, and the rosy-cheeked maid with the mole on her left temple – to him they had all withdrawn into the realm of ghosts. And although this made him shudder a little, there was also something soothing about this feeling, which seemed to release him from all responsibility, indeed from all connection with humanity.

One of the strolling girls was on the point of propositioning him. She was a pretty creature, still quite young but very pale with lips painted red. This could also end in death, he thought, only not *quite* so quickly! *Cowardice* again? Basically, yes. He heard her steps and then her voice behind him. 'Won't you come with me, doctor?'

Almost against his will, he turned around. 'How do you know me?' he asked.

'I don't know you,' she said, 'but in this district everyone's a doctor.'

He had not had anything to do with women of her kind since his high school days. If he were suddenly transported back to his boyhood, would this creature have attracted him? He remembered a passing acquaintance, an elegant young man who was reputed to be a great womanizer, with whom as a student he had once visited a nightclub after a ball, and how as he departed with one of the professional hostesses he answered Fridolin's bewildered look by saying, 'It's always the most pleasurable way. Besides, they're not the worst women in the world.'

'What's your name?' asked Fridolin.

'Mizzi, of course, what else?'

She had already turned the key in the door to the apartment block, and stepping into the entrance-hall she waited for Fridolin to follow her.

'Hurry up!' she said, as he hesitated. Suddenly he was standing next to her, the door fell to behind him, and having locked it she lit a candle and went on ahead to light the way. Am I mad? he asked himself. I won't touch her, of course.

An oil lamp was burning in the room. She turned up the wick: it was quite a comfortable room, well maintained, and at least it smelled more agreeable than Marianne's quarters, for instance. Admittedly, there had not been an old man lying here sick for

months. The girl smiled and without being impor-
tunate moved closer to Fridolin, who gently evaded
her. Then she pointed to a rocking-chair, which he
settled into readily.

'You must be very tired,' she said. He nodded. And
undressing without haste she went on, 'Ah, well, a man
like you, with all the things you have to see to all day
long. In that respect people like us have it easier.'

He noticed that her lips were not made up but
were a natural red, and complimented her on them.

'But why should I use make-up?' she asked. 'How
old do you think I am?'

'Twenty?' Fridolin guessed.

'Seventeen,' she said, and seated herself on his
lap, throwing her arm round his neck like a child.

Who in the world would guess, he thought, that
right now I'm here in a room like this of all places?
Would I myself have believed it possible an hour, or
even ten minutes ago? And – what for? Whatever
for? She sought his lips with hers, but he drew back,
and she looked at him with large, rather sad eyes and
slipped down off his lap. He almost felt regret, as
there had been a comforting tenderness in her
embrace.

She picked up a red dressing-gown lying over the back of the bed, which was made-up and ready, slipped into it and crossed her arms over her breasts so that her figure was entirely hidden.

'Is that better?' she asked without mockery, almost shyly, as if she were trying to understand him. He hardly knew what to reply.

'You've guessed right,' he said then. 'I'm really tired, and I find it very pleasant just sitting here in the rocking-chair and listening to you. You've such a sweet voice. Go on, talk to me, tell me something.'

She sat down on the bed and shook her head. 'You're afraid,' she said quietly – and then, almost inaudibly, gazing straight ahead, 'What a pity!'

These last words sent a warm current surging through his blood. He went over to her and attempted to embrace her, reassuring her that she inspired complete confidence in him, and indeed this was no more than the truth. He drew her to him and started to make love to her as he might to an ordinary girl or a woman that he loved. She resisted, and feeling ashamed he eventually desisted.

Then she said, 'One never knows, sooner or later it's bound to happen. You're quite right to be afraid. And if anything were to happen, you would curse me.'

She refused the banknote he offered her so resolutely that he did not press her further. She wrapped a narrow blue shawl around her, lit a candle to light the way for him, and accompanied him downstairs to unlock the door. 'I'm going to stay at home tonight,' she said. Involuntarily he took her hand and kissed it. She looked up at him astonished, almost frightened, then gave an embarrassed happy laugh. 'Just like a proper lady,' she said.

The door fell shut behind him, and Fridolin, with a quick glance, memorized the house number so that he could send wine and food up to the poor creature the following day.

IV

In the interim it had become even warmer. A gentle
breeze brought the scent of watery meadows and
spring in the distant mountains down into the narrow
street. Where to now? thought Fridolin, as though it
were not at all self-evident that he should at last go
home and sleep. Somehow he could not make up his
mind to do so. Strange how homeless, how rejected
he felt since that disagreeable encounter with the
Alemannic students . . . Or was it since Marianne's
confession? No, earlier still – indeed, ever since his
evening conversation with Albertine he had been
moving away from the habitual sphere of his existence, into some other remote and unfamiliar world.

He wandered up and down the nocturnal streets,
letting the light föhn wind play about his temples,
until at last, with a resolute stride, as though he had
reached a long-sought goal, he entered a modest

coffee-house, cosy in an old Viennese way, not particularly spacious, moderately lit and little frequented at that hour.

In a corner three gentlemen were playing cards; a waiter who until then had been watching them helped Fridolin out of his fur coat, took his order, and placed magazines and evening papers before him on the table. With a feeling of comfort and security, Fridolin began to leaf through the papers. Here and there an item caught his eye. In some Bohemian town German-language street-signs had been torn down. In Constantinople there was a conference on railway-building schemes in Asia Minor, in which Lord Cranford was also taking part. The firm of Benies & Weingruber had gone bankrupt. A prostitute named Anna Tiger had doused her friend Hermine Drobitzky with vitriol in a fit of jealousy. That evening a herring junket would take place in the Sophia Rooms. A young woman, one Maria B. of No. 28 Schönbrunner Hauptstrasse, had poisoned herself with sublimate. – Somehow all these sad or trivial events had a calming and sobering effect on Fridolin in their dry, everyday ordinariness. He felt sorry for the young Maria B. – sublimate, how stupid! At that very moment, while he was sitting comfortably in the café, and Albertine sleeping peacefully with her arms tucked behind her neck, and the Court Counsellor was beyond all earthly cares, Maria B. of No. 28 Schönbrunner Hauptstrasse was writhing senselessly in agony.

He looked up from the paper and became conscious of someone eyeing him from the table opposite. Nachtigall? Could it be? The other man had already recognized him, and, raising both arms in a gesture of agreeable surprise, came over to him – a large, broad, almost burly fellow, youngish still, with long wavy fair hair already streaked with grey and a drooping moustache after the Polish fashion. He wore an open grey coat over a slightly greasy evening suit, a creased shirt with three synthetic diamond buttons, a crumpled collar and a flapping white silk tie. His eyelids were red from many sleepless nights, but his blue eyes gleamed merrily.

'So you're in Vienna?' cried Fridolin.

'You didn't know,' said Nachtigall in a soft Polish accent with a slight Jewish intonation. 'How come you didn't know? Considering how famous I am.' He laughed aloud good-humouredly and sat down opposite Fridolin.

'How have you managed that?' asked Fridolin. 'Perhaps you've become Professor of Surgery on the quiet?'

Nachtigall laughed even more heartily. 'Didn't you hear me just now?'

'How do you mean, hear you? – Ah, I see!' And for the first time Fridolin became conscious of the fact that, as he had entered, indeed even earlier as he had approached the coffee-house, he had heard a piano playing from somewhere in the depths of the establishment. 'So that was you?' he exclaimed.

'Who else?' laughed Nachtigall.

Fridolin nodded. Yes, of course – that peculiarly energetic touch, those strange, somewhat haphazard yet melodious chords with the left hand had immediately seemed so familiar to him. 'So you've devoted yourself entirely to music?' he inquired. He recalled that Nachtigall had finally given up medicine after the second preliminary examination in zoology, which he had passed successfully but only after seven years. Yet he had continued for some time to hang about the hospital's dissecting room, laboratories and lecture halls, where, with his artist's shock of fair hair, his invariably crumpled collar, his fluttering once-white tie, he had been a striking, in a light-hearted sense popular, and even perhaps a beloved figure, not only among his peers but with some of the professors. The son of a Jewish dram-shop owner in a Polish backwater, he had in due course reached Vienna from his home town to study medicine. From the outset the allowance from his parents had been negligible, and in any case it had soon been revoked, but this did not prevent him continuing to appear at the get-togethers of one of the medical associations in the Riedhof to which Fridolin too belonged. Payment of his dues had at some stage been taken over in turn by one or other of his more affluent colleagues. Sometimes he was also offered gifts of clothing, which he accepted willingly and with no false pride. He had already learned the rudiments of piano-playing in his home town from a pianist stranded there, and while a medical student in Vienna he simultaneously attended the Conservatory, where apparently he was regarded as a talented and promising pianist. But here too he was not serious or industrious enough to develop his gifts systematically; and he soon contented himself with musical success only in his own immediate circle of acquaintances, or rather with the pleasure his piano-playing gave them.

For a time he was engaged as pianist in a suburban dancing-school. Fellow students from the university and medical fraternity tried to introduce him to the better houses in the same capacity, but on such occasions he would only play what he wanted and for as long as he wanted, he would engage young ladies in conversations which were not on his part always innocently pursued, and he would drink more than he could hold. On one occasion he played at a dance in the house of a bank-manager. Well before midnight, having embarrassed the young girls and offended their consorts with his risqué gallantries as they danced past, he took it into his head to play a wild cancan while singing couplets full of innuendoes in his powerful bass voice. The bank-manager rebuked him strongly. In rapturous high spirits, Nachtigall got up and embraced the manager, who was so appalled that, though himself a Jew, he hissed a Jewish insult in his face, to which Nachtigall promptly responded by boxing him soundly over the ears – and with this his career in the better houses of the city seemed to close for ever. In more intimate circles he generally managed to behave more decently, though even on such occasions he would sometimes in the small hours have to be forcibly removed from the premises. Yet the next morning such incidents were forgiven and forgotten by those involved. – One day, long after his contemporaries had completed their studies, he had suddenly left town without taking leave of anyone. For a few months greetings cards from him continued to arrive from various towns in Russia and Poland; and once, without further explanation, Fridolin, of whom Nachtigall had always been particularly fond, was reminded of his existence not merely by a greeting but by a request for a moderate sum of money. Fridolin sent off the money at once, but never received any thanks or further sign of life from Nachtigall.

And now, at quarter to one in the morning eight years later, Nachtigall insisted on making good this oversight, and proceeded to take precisely the right number of banknotes from a wallet which, though somewhat the worse for wear, appeared tolerably well lined, so that Fridolin felt able to accept the repayment in good conscience.

'You appear to be doing all right,' he observed smiling, as if to put his own mind at rest.

'Can't complain,' replied Nachtigall. And then, laying his hand on Fridolin's arm, 'But now tell me, what brings you here in the middle of the night?' Fridolin explained that his presence so late at night was the result of an urgent need for a cup of coffee after a nocturnal consultation; he did not say, however, without quite knowing why, that he had not found his patient alive. Then he talked in a general way about his medical activities at the clinic and his private practice, and mentioned that he was happily married and the father of a six-year-old girl.

Then Nachtigall told his story. As Fridolin had correctly surmised, he had spent all these years as a pianist in various Polish, Romanian, Serbian and Bulgarian towns and villages, and had a wife and four children living in Lemberg – here he laughed out loud, as though it were exceptionally amusing to have four children, all in Lemberg and all by one and the same woman. Since last autumn he had again been living in Vienna. The variety theatre that had engaged him had almost at once gone bankrupt, and now he was playing in different night-clubs as the occasion arose, sometimes even in two or three on the same night, like down here for instance in this basement tavern – hardly an elegant establishment, he observed, more like a bowling-alley, really, and as for the clientele . . . 'But when one has to provide for a wife and four children in Lemberg' – and he laughed again, not quite as heartily as before. 'Sometimes I also do some private work,' he added hastily. And he said, as he noticed the smile of recollection on Fridolin's face, 'Not with bank-managers and their ilk, no, in all sorts of circles, some of them more fashionable, some open and some secret.'

'Secret?'

Nachtigall looked straight ahead with a gloomy, knowing expression. 'They'll be picking me up shortly.'

'What, you're performing again tonight?'

'Yes, these things never start before two o'clock.'

'Well, that sounds splendid,' said Fridolin.

'Yes and no,' laughed Nachtigall, but he immediately became serious again.

'Yes and no?' repeated Fridolin curiously.

'I'm playing at a private house tonight, but don't know whose.'

'So you're playing for them for the first time?' asked Fridolin with mounting interest.

'No, for the third time. But it will probably be yet another house.'

'I don't understand.'

'Neither do I,' laughed Nachtigall. 'You'd better stop asking questions.'

'Hmm,' said Fridolin.

'Oh, you're mistaken. It's not what you think. I've seen quite a lot, things you wouldn't believe in such small towns – especially in Romania – but one lives and learns. Here however . . .' He drew the yellow curtain back a little, looked out on to the street and, as if to himself, said, 'Not there yet,' saying by way of explanation to Fridolin, 'I mean the coach. I'm always picked up by a coach, and it's a different one each time.'

'You make me curious, Nachtigall,' remarked Fridolin coolly.

'Listen,' said Nachtigall after some hesitation. 'If there's anyone in the world I'd do a favour for – but how would we go about it,' adding suddenly, 'Do you have the courage?'

'What a question,' said Fridolin in the tone of an insulted fraternity student.

'I didn't mean it like that.'

'Well, how did you mean it exactly? What's so special about this occasion that requires such courage? What could happen to me anyway?' And he gave a short, contemptuous laugh.

'Nothing could happen to *me,* or at worst this might be my last engagement – but that may be the case regardless.' He fell silent and again looked out through the gap in the curtains.

'Well then?'

'How do you mean?' asked Nachtigall, as if summoned from a dream.

'Tell me more. Now you've started . . . Secret shows? Closed societies? Invited guests?'

'I don't know much about it. Most recently there were thirty people, the first time only sixteen.'

'A ball?'

'A ball, of course.' He now seemed to regret ever having spoken.

'And you provide the music for it?'

'How d'you mean: for it? I don't know what it's for. I really don't. I simply keep on playing – but with my eyes blindfolded.'

'Come, now, Nachtigall, what sort of song is this you're singing me!'

Nachtigall sighed softly. 'Well, not completely blindfolded, admittedly. Not so that I can't see anything at all. That is, I can see things in the mirror through the black silk scarf tied over my eyes . . .' And again he paused.

'In a word,' said Fridolin impatiently and a little scornfully but feeling strangely excited, 'naked females.'

'Don't call them females, Fridolin,' replied Nachtigall in an offended tone, 'you've never seen such women.'

Fridolin cleared his throat lightly. 'And how high is the entrance fee?' he asked casually.

'You mean tickets and all that? Whatever are you thinking of?'

'Well, how does one get admittance, then?' asked Fridolin tight-lipped, drumming on the table.

'You have to know the password, and it's different each time.'

'And what about today?'

'I don't know it yet. Not until I get it from the coachman.'

'Take me with you, Nachtigall.'

'Impossible. Too dangerous.'

'But a moment ago you yourself were prepared to . . . do me "the favour". It shouldn't really be impossible.'

Nachtigall looked him over critically. 'The way you are now – you couldn't get in under any circumstances, since both gentlemen and ladies all wear masks. You don't happen to have a mask and so on with you? Hardly likely . . . Well, next time, perhaps. I'll think of something.' He pricked up his ears and again looked out on to the street through the gap in the curtains, and, taking a deep breath, said, 'There's the coach. Adieu.'

Fridolin gripped him firmly by the arm. 'I won't let you get out of it like this. You're going to take me with you.'

'But–'

'Leave everything else to me. I know it's dangerous – perhaps that's exactly what attracts me.'

'But I've already told you, without a mask and costume –'

'There are places one can hire a mask.'

'At one in the morning!'

'Now listen, Nachtigall. There's just such an outfitter's on the corner of the Wickenburgstrasse. I pass the sign several times a day.' And in mounting excitement he continued hurriedly, 'You wait here for another quarter of an hour, while I try my luck with them. The owner of the shop may well live in the same building. If not – well then, I'll simply have to forgo the whole adventure. Let fate decide. In the same house there's a café, I believe it's called the Café Vindobona. Tell the coachman you've forgotten something there, and when you enter – I'll be waiting near the door – quickly give me the password and get back into your cab; if I've managed to get a costume, I'll take another cab and follow you at once – the rest must take care of itself. In any case, I'll shoulder all responsibility for the risk you're taking, Nachtigall, upon my word of honour.'

Nachtigall had attempted to interrupt Fridolin several times, but to no avail. Fridolin flung the money for the bill on to the table, including an overly generous tip, which seemed to him in keeping with the tone of the entire evening, and departed. A closed coach was standing outside, the coachman in a top hat sitting motionless on the box – like a hearse, thought Fridolin. After a few minutes' brisk walk he reached the corner house in question, rang, and inquired of the porter whether Herr Gibiser the costumier lived in the same building, secretly hoping this would prove not to be the case. But Gibiser did in fact live there, on the floor below the outfitter's establishment. Nor did the porter seem particularly surprised at the late visit; indeed, being in an affable mood after Fridolin's handsome tip, he remarked that during the Shrovetide Carnival season it was by no means uncommon for people to come by as late as this to rent out costumes. He lit up the stairwell with a candle from below until Fridolin had rung the door-bell on the first floor. Herr Gibiser himself opened up at once, as if he had been waiting behind the door: he was gaunt, beardless and bald, and wore an old-fashioned floral dressing-gown and a tassled Turkish fez, so that he looked like a comic elder in a play. Fridolin made his request, saying that the price was of no consequence, to which Mr Gibiser replied dismissively, 'I ask what's owing to me, nothing more.'

He led Fridolin up a spiral staircase to the storeroom. There was a pervasive smell of silk, satin, perfume, dust and dry flowers; here and there in the

looming darkness red and silvery objects glinted;
then suddenly a string of little lights came on between
the lockers of a long narrow gallery stretching back
into the gloom. To the left and right of them costumes
of every imaginable kind were hanging: on one side
there were knights, squires, peasants, huntsmen,
sages, orientals, fools; on the other, maids of honour,
courtly ladies, peasant women, chambermaids and
queens-of-the-night. Appropriate headgear was on
display above the costumes, so that Fridolin felt as
though he were walking down an avenue of gallows-
birds on the point of asking one another for a dance.
Herr Gibiser followed along behind him. 'Have you
any particular preference, sir? *Louis Quatorze? Direc-
toire?* Old Germanic?'

'I want a dark monk's habit and a black mask,
that's all.'

At that moment a sound of glasses clinking came
from the end of the gallery. Startled, Fridolin looked
at the costumier, as though he owed him an immediate
explanation. Gibiser had stopped short, however, and
was reaching for some hidden switch – immediately
a dazzling light spread to the far end of the gallery,
where a small table decked with plates, glasses and

bottles could be seen. Two masked figures in the red robes of vehmic court judges rose from their chairs to the left and right of it, while simultaneously a glittering dainty creature disappeared from sight. Taking long strides, Gibiser rushed towards them, reached across the table and snatched up a white wig, while at the same time a charming young girl, still almost a child, wearing a Pierrette's costume and white silk stockings, wriggled out from under it and came running down the gallery to Fridolin, who was thus obliged to receive her in his arms. Gibiser had dropped the wig on to the table and was holding the two judges on either side of him firmly by their pleated robes. At the same time he called out to Fridolin, 'Hold on to the girl for me there, sir!' The little creature snuggled close to Fridolin, as though seeking his protection. Her narrow face was powdered white and adorned with several beauty spots, and a scent of roses and powder emanated from her tender breasts, while her eyes twinkled with mischief and desire.

'Gentlemen,' cried Gibiser, 'you will remain here until I hand you over to the police.'

'What on earth are you thinking of?' they both exclaimed. And, as if from one mouth, 'We were merely responding to an invitation from your little Fräulein.'

Gibiser let go of them and Fridolin heard him say, 'You'll have to give a better account of yourselves than that. Didn't you see straight away that you were dealing with a madwoman?' Turning to Fridolin, he said, 'My apologies, sir, for this little incident.'

'Oh, no harm done,' said Fridolin. What he would have liked most was to stay on there, or failing that to have taken the girl away with him at once, wherever – or whatever the consequences. She gazed up at him enticingly, and yet like a child, as if under his spell. The judges at the end of the gallery were talking animatedly to one another, and Gibiser turned to Fridolin in a businesslike manner and asked, 'You wanted a cowl, sir, a pilgrim's hat, a mask?'

'No,' said the little Pierrette with shining eyes, 'you must give this gentleman an ermine mantle and a red silk jerkin.'

'Don't you dare move from my side,' said Gibiser and, pointing to a monk's cowl hanging between the costumes of a yeoman and a Venetian senator, observed, 'This should be your size, sir, here's the matching hat, take them quickly, now!'

Here the judges again came forward. 'You must let us out at once, Herr Ghibisier,' they said, to Fridolin's surprise giving the name Gibiser its French pronunciation.

'There can be no question of that,' replied the costumier scornfully, 'and for the moment you'll be so kind as to wait here till I return.'

Meanwhile Fridolin slipped on the cowl, tying the ends of the trailing white cord into a knot, while Gibiser, standing on a narrow ladder, handed down a black, broad-brimmed pilgrim's hat which Fridolin also put on; yet he did all this as if under compulsion, feeling more and more obliged to stand by the little Pierrette, should any danger threaten her. The mask which Gibiser now handed to him, and which he immediately tried on, smelled of an exotic, slightly unpleasant perfume.

'You go on ahead of me,' said Gibiser to the young girl, pointing firmly in the direction of the stairs. The little Pierrette turned towards the far end of the gallery and gaily waved a sad farewell. Fridolin followed her gaze and beheld not two vehmic court judges as before, but two slim young gentlemen in white ties and evening dress, though both were still wearing the red masks over their faces. Then the Pierrette swung down the spiral staircase. Gibiser went next and Fridolin followed on behind. In the hall below Gibiser opened the door leading to the inner rooms and said to the Pierrette, 'Go straight to bed, you depraved young creature, I'll deal with you as soon as I've settled matters with the gentlemen upstairs.'

She stood in the door, white and slender, and, with a glance at Fridolin, sadly shook her head. In a large wall-mirror to the right Fridolin caught sight of a gaunt-looking pilgrim, none other than himself, and marvelled at how natural all this seemed. The little Pierrette had vanished and the old costumier locked the door behind her. Then he opened the door of the apartment and hurried Fridolin out into the main stairwell.

'Excuse me,' said Fridolin, 'what do I owe you?'

'Don't worry, sir, you can pay when you return them; I trust you.'

But Fridolin did not move. 'Will you give me your word that you'll not do the poor child any harm?'

'What business is that of yours, sir?'

'I heard you refer to the girl as mad before, and

just now you called her a depraved young creature. A remarkable contradiction, wouldn't you agree?'

'Well, sir,' replied Gibiser in a censorious tone, 'aren't the mad depraved in the eyes of God?'

Fridolin shook himself angrily. 'However that may be,' he observed, 'it should be possible to get professional advice. I'm a doctor. Tomorrow we'll talk the matter over further.'

Gibiser gave a soundless scornful laugh. In the stairwell a light suddenly went on, the door between Gibiser and Fridolin closed, and the bolt was immediately thrust home. As he went downstairs, Fridolin took off the hat, cowl and mask, and put them under his arm. When the porter opened the door on to the street, the 'hearse' with the driver bolt upright on the box was waiting opposite. Nachtigall was on the point of leaving the café, and did not seem too pleased that Fridolin was there on time after all.

'So you've really managed to get yourself fitted out?'

'As you see. And the password?'

'So you insist?'

'Absolutely.'

'Well then – the password's "Denmark".'

'Nachtigall, you must be mad!'

'What do you mean, mad?'

'Oh, nothing, nothing. It just so happens that I was on the Danish coast last summer. Well, get in – but take your time, so that I have a chance to pick up a cab over there.'

Nachtigall nodded and slowly lit a cigarette, while Fridolin rapidly crossed the street, engaged a cab and in a light-hearted tone, as though participating in some prank, directed his driver to follow the hearse just setting off in front of them.

They drove along the Alserstrasse and then under a railway viaduct out towards the suburbs, passing through ill-lit side-streets with nobody about. Fridolin considered the possibility that his driver might lose sight of the coach ahead; but whenever he stuck his head out of the window into the unnaturally warm air, he could still see the other coach a little distance in front, and the coachman in his tall black top hat sitting motionless on the box. It could all end disastrously, thought Fridolin. Yet he was still conscious of the scent of roses and powder that had emanated from the little Pierrette's breasts. What strange adventure did I brush past there? he asked himself. Perhaps

I shouldn't have left, perhaps it was my duty not to. Where am I now, I wonder?

They were climbing steadily past modest villas. Fridolin thought he could now make out where they were. Years ago he had sometimes found his way up here on walks: this, surely, was the Galitzinberg that they were climbing. Far down to the left, floating in the haze, he could see the city gleaming with a thousand lights. Then, hearing the sound of wheels behind them, he looked back out of the window. Two coaches were following them, and this pleased him, since now the driver of the hearse could not possibly be suspicious of him.

Suddenly, with a violent jolt, the coach turned off into a side-road, and they went hurtling down between fences, walls and ridges as if into a ravine. It occurred to Fridolin that it was high time he disguised himself. He took off his fur coat and slipped on the cowl, exactly as he would slip into the sleeves of his linen coat each morning in the hospital; and, as though this might somehow redeem him, he reflected that, if all went well, in a few hours he would be going about between his patients' beds as he did every morning – a doctor ready to be of service.

The coach came to a halt. Suppose, thought Fridolin, I didn't get out at all – and drove back at once instead? But where to? To the little Pierrette? Or to the little trollop in the Buchfeldgasse? Or to Marianne, the daughter of the dead Court Counsellor? Or home? And with a slight shudder he realized that there was nowhere he wanted to go less. Or was it because that path seemed more circuitous to him? No, I can't go back, he thought to himself. My way lies forward, even were it to my death. He couldn't help laughing at these melodramatic notions, but even so he did not feel altogether at his ease.

There was a garden gate standing wide open. The hearse in front of him drove on further down into the ravine, or, as it seemed to him, into the dark abyss. Evidently Nachtigall had already alighted. Fridolin hastily climbed out of his carriage and instructed the coachman to wait at the corner for his return, however long that might be. And to secure his further services, he paid him handsomely in advance, promising him an equal fee for the return ride. The coaches that had followed his drew up, and from the first of these Fridolin glimpsed a veiled female figure getting out. Lowering his mask, he went into the garden, where a narrow path illuminated from the house led to the front door: its two wings sprang open and Fridolin found himself in a narrow white hallway. The sound of a harmonium reached his ears, and on either side two servants in dark livery were standing, their faces hidden behind grey masks.

'The password?' they whispered in chorus, and he answered, 'Denmark'. One of the servants took charge of his fur coat and disappeared with it into an adjacent room, the other opened a door and Fridolin entered a dark, dimly lit, high-ceilinged room, draped with black silk hangings. Some sixteen to twenty masked revellers, all dressed in the ecclesiastical apparel of either monks or nuns, were strolling up and down. The softly resonant tones of the harmonium, playing an old Italian sacred tune, seemed to descend as if from on high. In one corner of the room stood a small group of people, three nuns and two monks, who had been looking round at him rather pointedly and then quickly turning away. Noticing that he was the only one with his head still covered, Fridolin took off his pilgrim's hat and strolled up and down, trying to seem as innocent as possible. A monk touched him on the arm and nodded a greeting, but for just a second his gaze bored deep into Fridolin's eyes from behind his mask. A strange, sultry fragrance enveloped him, as if from southern gardens. Again someone touched him on the arm. This time it was a nun. Like the others she had covered her brow, head and neck with a black veil, and her blood-red mouth glistened beneath her black lace mask. Where am I? thought Fridolin. Among madmen? Among conspirators? Have I strayed into a gathering of some religious sect? Had Nachtigall perhaps been ordered, or paid, to bring someone uninitiated for them to have a bit of fun with? Yet for a prank at a masked ball it all seemed far too earnest, too monotonous and too eerie. A female voice now accompanied the sound of the harmonium, and an old Italian religious canticle resounded through the room. Everyone stood still and seemed to be listening, and Fridolin too surrendered for a while to the marvellous swelling melody. Suddenly a female voice behind him whispered, 'Don't turn round. There's still time for you to leave. You don't belong here. If they were to discover you, you'd be in serious trouble.'

Fridolin started. For an instant he considered heeding the warning. But curiosity, temptation and above all pride were stronger than all other considerations. I've come this far, he thought, let things take what course they will. And without turning round he shook his head in flat refusal.

Then the voice behind him whispered, 'Well, for your sake, I'm sorry.'

At this point he turned round. He could clearly make out the blood-red mouth gleaming behind the lace veil, and dark eyes sinking into his. 'I'm staying,' he said in a heroic voice he did not recognize as his own, and turned away again. The singing was rising to a splendid climax, but quite different sounds were now issuing from the harmonium, not at all in the religious mode, but worldly, sensuous and booming like an organ; and looking around Fridolin noticed that all the nuns had disappeared and only monks were left in the room. Meanwhile the voice of the singer too had modulated from gloomy solemnity via an artfully ascending trill into a mood of levity and jubilation. In place of the harmonium a piano had struck up a more impudent and earthy note, and Fridolin immediately recognized Nachtigall's wild and rousing touch, while the female voice, hitherto so noble, culminated in a shrill, lascivious screech which seemed to take off through the roof into infinity. Doors on either side opened, and through one set Fridolin recognized the shadowy outline of Nachtigall's figure at the piano, while the room opposite was suffused with dazzling light, and there the ladies were standing motionless, each with a dark veil covering her head, brow and neck, and a black lace mask over her face, but otherwise completely naked. Fridolin's eyes roved hungrily from sensuous to slender figures, and from budding figures to figures in glorious full bloom; and the fact that each of these naked beauties still remained a mystery, and that from behind the masks large eyes as unfathomable as riddles sparkled at him, transformed his indescribably strong urge to watch into an almost intolerable torment of desire. The other men were evidently experiencing much the same as he was. The first moments of breathtaking delight gave way to sighs of deep distress; a cry escaped from someone; and then suddenly, as if they were being chased, they all charged, now no longer in their monkish cowls but dressed in festive white, yellow, blue or crimson courtiers' clothes, out of the dimly lit room towards the women, where they were received with insane, almost sinister laughter. Fridolin was the only one left behind still dressed as a monk, and he slunk off a little apprehensively into a remote corner, where he found himself close to Nachtigall, who had his back to him. Fridolin could see that Nachtigall had been blindfolded, but he also thought he noticed that beneath the cloth his eyes were riveted to the tall mirror opposite, where the gaudy courtiers swirled with their naked dancing-partners.

Suddenly one of the women was standing next to Fridolin and whispered – for no one spoke a word aloud, as though their voices too must remain a secret – 'Why so lonely? Won't you join the dance?'

Fridolin noticed that two noblemen were eyeing him sharply from the other corner, and he suspected that the creature at his side – she was slim of build and boyish – had been sent to test and entice him. Despite this he extended his arms towards her and was about to draw her to him, when one of the other women disengaged herself from her dancing-partner and came running over towards Fridolin. He realized at once that it was the person who had warned him earlier. She pretended she had just caught sight of him for the first time, and whispered, though

sufficiently distinctly for them to have heard her in
the other corner, 'So you're back at last?' And laughing gaily, 'It's no use, you've been recognized.' And
turning to the boyish woman, 'Leave him to me for
just two minutes. Then you can have him again, until
morning if you wish.' And then more softly to her,
and as if elated, 'It's him, yes, him.' With surprise,
the other woman said, 'Really?' and glided off to join
the courtiers in the other corner.

'Don't ask questions,' said the one who had
remained behind with Fridolin, 'and don't be astonished at anything. I've done my best to mislead her,
but I can tell you now: it won't succeed for long. Fly
while there's time. Any minute it could simply be too
late. Make sure too that they don't follow your tracks.
No one must discover who you are. It would be the
end of your tranquillity, of your peace of mind, for
ever. Go!'

'Will I see you again?'

'Impossible.'

'Then I'm staying.'

A shudder went through her naked body, transmit-
ting itself to him and almost depriving him of his
senses.

'No more than my life can be at stake,' he said, 'and to me at this moment you're worth it.' He seized her hands and tried to draw her to him.

Again, as if in despair, she whispered, 'Go!'

He laughed and could hear himself as one hears oneself in dreams. 'I know exactly where I am. You're not here, all of you, simply to arouse by your appearance. You're deliberately playing games with me, so as to drive me completely mad.'

'It will be too late, go!'

But he refused to listen to her. 'Are there no discreet apartments here, where couples who have discovered one another can retire? Are all those assembled here going to take leave of their partners with a polite kiss of the hand? It doesn't look like it.'

And he pointed to the reflection in the mirror of the brilliantly lit adjacent room, where the couples were dancing to the frantic strains of the piano, gleaming white bodies pressed against blue, red and yellow silk. He had the feeling that now no one was paying any attention to him and the woman by his side, as they stood there alone in the middle room in almost total darkness.

'Your hopes are vain,' she whispered. 'There are

no apartments here, such as you imagine. You don't have a minute to spare. Fly!'

'Come with me.'

She shook her head violently, as if in desperation.

He laughed again and couldn't recognize his laugh. 'You can't be serious. Have these men and women come here just to arouse and then to scorn each other? Who can forbid you to leave with me, if you so wish?'

She took a deep breath and lowered her head.

'Ah, now I understand,' he said. 'So this is the punishment you reserve for anyone who slips in uninvited. You could scarcely have conceived of a more cruel one. Release me from it. Have mercy on me. Impose some other penance. Only don't force me to depart without you!'

'You're mad. I can't leave with you, any more than – with anybody else. And anyone who tried to follow me would be forfeiting both his life and mine.'

Fridolin was intoxicated, and not merely by her presence, her fragrant body and burning red lips, nor by the atmosphere of the room and the aura of lascivious secrets that surrounded him; he was at once thirsty and delirious, made so by all the adventures of the night, none of which had led to anything, by his own audacity, and by the sea-change he felt within himself. He stretched out and touched the veil covering her head, as though intending to remove it.

She seized his hands. 'One night someone did take it into his head during the dance to strip the veil from one of us. They tore off his mask and drove him out with a whip.'

'And – what happened to her?'

'You may have read about a beautiful young girl – it was only a few weeks ago – who took poison the day before her marriage.'

He even remembered the name and mentioned it. Hadn't it been a girl from an aristocratic family, engaged to an Italian prince?

She nodded.

Suddenly one of the courtiers was standing beside them, the most resplendent of them all and the only one in white; and with a curt but polite if somewhat imperious bow, he invited the woman with whom Fridolin was speaking to dance. Fridolin had the impression that she hesitated for a moment. But already the man had put his arm round her and was waltzing away with her towards the other couples in the adjacent lighted room.

Now Fridolin found himself alone, and this sudden abandonment descended on him like a frost. He looked around. For the moment no one seemed in the least concerned about him. Perhaps there was still one last chance that he might escape unpunished. What it was that despite this held him spellbound in his corner, invisible and unobserved – whether it was fear of an ignoble and somewhat ridiculous retreat, or the torment of unsatisfied longing for the mysterious woman's body, whose fragrance still caressed him, or the notion that everything he had seen so far might have been meant to test his courage, and that the gorgeous woman would fall to him as his reward – he did not rightly know himself. At all events, it was clear to him that this suspense was no longer tolerable, and that no matter what the danger he must bring the situation to a head. Whatever he decided, it could scarcely be a matter of life and death. He might be among fools and perhaps even among profligates, but certainly not among criminals and thugs. And the thought occurred to him that he might go over and join them, acknowledge that he was an intruder, and place himself chivalrously at their disposal. This seemed the only possible way to end the night, with an honourable understanding, as it were – if, that is, it were to be anything more than a barren, shadowy succession of dreary, lurid and scurrilous libidinous adventures, none of which had been pursued to the end. And with a deep breath he prepared himself.

At that very moment, however, someone beside him whispered, 'The password!' A courtier dressed in black had suddenly approached him, and since Fridolin did not answer straight away he asked a second time.

'Denmark,' replied Fridolin.

'Quite right, sir, that is the password for the entrance. The password to the house, if you wouldn't mind?'

Fridolin said nothing.

'Would you be so good as to give us the password to the house?' It sounded sharp as a knife. Fridolin shrugged his shoulders. The other man stepped into the middle of the room and raised his hand, whereupon the piano fell silent and the dance came to a halt. Two other courtiers, one in yellow, the other in blue, came up. 'The password, sir,' they both said at once.

'I've forgotten it,' replied Fridolin with a vacant smile, feeling totally at ease.

'That's unfortunate,' said the gentleman in yellow, 'for it makes no difference here whether you've forgotten the password, or whether you never knew it.'

The other male masked revellers crowded in and the doors on either side were closed. Fridolin stood there alone in his monk's cowl, surrounded by lavishly dressed courtiers.

'Take off your mask!' cried several of them at once. Fridolin held up his arm in front of him as if to shield his face. It seemed to him a thousand times worse to stand there as the only one unmasked amid a host of masks, than suddenly to stand naked among those fully dressed. And in a firm voice he said, 'If any of you gentlemen should feel his honour stained by my appearance here, I'm quite ready to give him satisfaction in the usual way. But I'll remove my mask only on the condition, gentlemen, that the rest of you do likewise.'

'It's not a question here of satisfaction,' said a courtier dressed in red, who had not spoken before, 'but of expiation.'

'Take off your mask!' repeated someone else with a clear, insolent voice which reminded Fridolin of an officer's peremptory command. 'You shall be told what awaits you to your face, not to your mask.'

'I'll not remove it,' said Fridolin even more sharply, 'and woe to him who dares lay hands on me.'

An arm suddenly snatched at his face, as if to tear off the mask, when all at once a door opened and a woman – Fridolin had no doubt who it was – stood there, in the habit of a nun, just as when he had first seen her. Behind her in the brilliantly lit room he could see the others, naked with their faces hidden, huddled together, silent, an intimidated group. But the door closed again immediately.

'Release him,' said the nun. 'I'm willing to redeem him.'

There was a moment of profound silence, as though something appalling had occurred, then the courtier in black who had first demanded the password from Fridolin turned to the nun and said, 'You're aware of what you're taking upon yourself?'

'Yes, I'm aware.'

Something like a collective gasp went through the room.

'You're free,' said the courtier to Fridolin. 'Leave the house at once, and beware of delving more deeply into secrets you've merely sneaked across the threshold of. Should you attempt to put anyone on our tracks, whether successfully or not – you'll be lost.'

Fridolin stood motionless. 'In what way is . . . this woman to redeem me?' he asked.

There was no answer. Several arms pointed towards the door, indicating that he should leave immediately.

Fridolin shook his head. 'You may impose what penalty you like on me, but I won't tolerate someone else paying for me.'

'You wouldn't alter anything of this woman's fate,' the courtier in black now said very softly. 'Here, once a pledge has been given, there's no going back.'

The nun nodded slowly as if in confirmation. 'Go!' she said to Fridolin.

'No,' he replied, raising his voice. 'Life is no longer worth anything to me if I have to leave without you. I don't ask where you come from, or who you might be. What difference can it make to you, unknown gentlemen, whether you play this Carnival comedy through to its conclusion, whether it was intended to end seriously? Whoever you may be, gentlemen, each of you leads another existence outside this one. I, however, am not playing a part, and if I have done so hitherto under duress, I now will cease to do so. I feel that I have found a destiny which has nothing to do with this charade, and I want to tell you my name, to remove my mask and to take all the consequences upon myself.'

'Beware!' the nun cried out, 'you would destroy yourself without saving me! Go!' And, turning to the others, 'Here I am, at your disposal – all of you!'

Her dark costume fell away from her as if by magic, so that she stood there in all the radiance of her white body, and, taking hold of the veil wound about her brow, head and neck, with a wonderful circular movement she removed it. It sank to the ground, and her dark hair cascaded over her shoulders, breast and hips – but before Fridolin managed to catch a glimpse of her face, he was seized by irresistibly strong arms, dragged away and thrust towards the door. A moment later he found himself in the hall, the door behind him closed, a masked servant brought him his fur coat and helped him into it, and the front door opened. As if propelled by some invisible force, he hurried out

and, regaining the street as the light went out behind
him, turned round and saw the house lying there in
silence, with not a glimmer of light escaping from the
closed windows. All I have to do is remember everything precisely, was his first thought. If I can find the
house again, everything else will follow in due course.

The night stretched all around him, but a little
further up where his coach was supposed to wait for
him a dim reddish light was shining. From the lower
end of the street the hearse appeared, as though he
had just summoned it. A servant opened the door.

'I have my own coach,' said Fridolin. The servant
shook his head. 'If it has driven away, I shall return
to the city on foot.'

The servant replied with a gesture which, far from
being servile, clearly brooked no opposition. In the
gloom the coachman's top hat seemed to loom
absurdly tall. The wind was blowing briskly and
violet clouds were racing across the sky. After all his
adventures thus far, Fridolin could not delude himself that he had any choice but to get into the
carriage, and it promptly moved off.

Fridolin felt determined, whatever the risk, to get
to the bottom of the whole affair as soon as it was

feasible. His existence, he felt, would no longer make sense if he failed to find the enigmatic woman, who at that same moment was paying the price of his release. What that would entail was all too easy to guess. But what could be her motive in sacrificing herself for him? Sacrifice ... Was she the sort of woman for whom what she was now facing, what she was preparing to submit to, would really constitute a sacrifice? If she was taking part in such gatherings – and today could scarcely be the first occasion, since she was so familiar with their rituals – what could it matter to her whether she submitted to the will of one or all of these courtiers? Could she be anything more than a cheap whore? What else could any of these women be? All whores without a doubt. Even if they lead a second, so-called bourgeois life alongside this one, it would still for all that be a whore's life. And wasn't everything he had just experienced in all probability an infamous jest they had indulged in at his expense? A jest that had been anticipated, prepared for and perhaps even built into the proceedings, in case an intruder should manage to sneak in? And yet when he thought about that woman who had warned him from the outset, and who was now prepared to ransom him – there had been something about her voice, her bearing and the nobility of her naked figure that could not possibly have been unauthentic. Or had his, Fridolin's, sudden appearance brought about some miraculous reformation in her? After everything he had experienced that night, he found it impossible – and he was not conscious of any affectation in the idea – to believe in such a miracle. But perhaps there are times, or nights, he thought, when some strange irresistible magic does emanate from men who under normal circumstances are not imbued with any particular power over the opposite sex?

The hearse continued to climb, even though in the normal course of events it should have turned into the main road long ago. What were they going to do with him? Where was the coach taking him? Was the comedy perhaps to have a sequel? Of what kind would it be? Would it have an enlightening resolution? A happy reunion somewhere else, perhaps? A reward for an initiation honourably endured and acceptance into the secret society? Undisturbed possession of the gorgeous nun? The carriage windows were all closed; Fridolin attempted to look out, but they were opaque. He tried to open the windows on either side but without success; and the glass partition between him and the coachman's box was just as opaque, just as firmly sealed. He knocked at the glass pane, shouted, screamed, but the coach rolled on. He tried to open first the door on the left-hand side and then on the right, but they simply would not yield, and his redoubled cries were lost amid the rumbling wheels and the whistling of the wind. The coach began to jolt as it drove downhill at an ever faster pace, and Fridolin, seized by anxiety and fear, was on the point of smashing one of the opaque windows when the carriage suddenly came to a halt. Both doors opened at once as though mechanically operated, now appearing ironically to give Fridolin the choice of alighting to either the right or the left. He leaped out of the coach, the doors slammed to, and, without the coachman paying Fridolin the slightest notice, the carriage drove off through the open fields into the night.

The sky was overcast, the clouds were scudding, the wind whistling, and Fridolin found himself standing in the snow, which emitted a faint radiance all about him. And as he stood there with his fur coat open over the monk's habit, the pilgrim's hat on his head, he felt a little eerie. The main highway was a short distance away. A procession of streetlights flickering wanly pointed the direction into town. But Fridolin set out straight ahead, taking a short-cut downhill across a fairly steep, snow-covered field, in order to mingle with other people again as rapidly as possible. With soaking feet he reached a narrow, badly lit street, and continued for a while between high board fences creaking in the wind; then, rounding the next corner, he emerged into a slightly wider street, where modest little houses alternated with vacant plots of land. A steeple clock struck three. Someone wearing a short jacket was coming towards Fridolin, his hands in his trouser pockets, his head tucked between his shoulders, his hat pressed low over his brow. Fridolin braced himself in readiness for an assault, but to his surprise the tramp did an about-turn and ran off. What was that all about, Fridolin asked himself. Then he remembered that his appearance must be more than a little uncanny. He took off his pilgrim's hat and buttoned up his overcoat, though below it the monk's habit still flapped about his ankles. Again he turned a corner, and, as he entered the main suburban street, a man in rural garb approached him and greeted him as one would a priest. The light from a street lamp fell across the street-sign on the corner house. Liebhartstal – so, not very far from the house he had left an hour ago. For a second he was tempted to take the road back and await developments nearby the house. But almost at once he gave up the idea, reflecting that he might well find himself in serious danger without coming any closer to solving the mystery. The thought of the things that might at that very moment be taking place inside the villa filled him with horror, despair, shame and fear. These reflections were so intolerable that Fridolin almost regretted he had not been set upon by the tramp, indeed almost regretted he was not lying against a fence in the backstreet with a knife between his ribs. That way this senseless night with its stupid, unresolved adventures might at least have made some sort of sense. Going home like this, as he was on the point of doing, seemed to him positively ridiculous. Yet so far nothing had been lost. Tomorrow was another day. And he vowed not to rest until he had again found the beautiful woman, whose dazzling nakedness had so mesmerized him. Only now did he think of Albertine – and felt as though he were obliged to conquer her as well, as though she could not, should not be his again until he had betrayed her with all the others he had met that night, with the naked woman, with the Pierrette, with Marianne, and with the little trollop from the narrow backstreet. Shouldn't he also perhaps attempt to track down the insolent student who had barged into him, and challenge him to fight it out with swords, or better still with pistols? What was another man's life to him, indeed, what was his own? Should one always risk it only out of duty or self-sacrifice, never on a whim, or out of passion or simply as a test of fate?

And again it crossed his mind that his body might already be carrying the seed of some fatal disease. Wouldn't it be absurd to die because a child infected with diphtheria had coughed in one's face? Perhaps he was already sick. Didn't he have a fever? Wasn't he perhaps lying at home in bed this very moment – and hadn't everything he believed he had experienced been nothing more than his delirium?

Fridolin opened his eyes as wide as he could, put his hand to his cheek and brow, and felt his pulse.

Scarcely above normal. Everything was fine. He was fully awake.

He continued on down the street towards the city. A few market carts came up behind him and rumbled past, and now and then he passed poorly clad people for whom the day had already begun. Behind a coffee-house window, at a table above which a gas light was flickering, a fat man with a scarf around his neck sat sleeping with his head in his hands. The houses still lay in darkness, and only a few isolated windows were lit up. Fridolin was aware of people gradually awakening, and imagined them in bed stretching and preparing to face their sour, miserable day. He too was faced with another day, but not with one that was miserable and dreary. And with a strange quickening of the heart he became agreeably conscious that within a few hours he would be going up and down in his white linen coat between his patients' beds. At the next corner a one-horse cab was waiting, the coachman asleep on the box: Fridolin woke him, gave him his address and climbed in.

V

It was four in the morning as he climbed the stairs to his apartment. The first thing he did was to go into his consulting-room and lock the mask and habit carefully away in a cupboard, and, as he wanted to avoid waking Albertine, took his shoes and clothes off before entering the bedroom. Carefully he turned up his bedside lamp. Albertine was lying quite still, her arms behind her neck, her half-open lips distressingly contorted by the play of shadows: it was a face unknown to Fridolin. He bent over her brow, which puckered at once as if in response to being touched, while her features became curiously distorted; then suddenly she laughed out loud so shrilly in her sleep that Fridolin was startled. Involuntarily he called out to her by name. As if in response, she laughed again in an utterly alien, almost uncanny manner. Fridolin called out to her more loudly. And now slowly and wearily her eyes opened wide, and she looked at him blankly as if she did not recognize him.

'Albertine!' he cried for the third time. Only then did she seem to come to her senses. An expression of revulsion and fear came into her eyes. She raised her arms in a futile and somehow desperate gesture, gaping at him open-mouthed.

'What's the matter?' asked Fridolin with bated breath. She continued to stare at him in horror, so he added soothingly, 'Albertine, it's me.' She took a deep breath, tried to smile and, letting her arms fall back on to the bed-cover, asked in a distant voice, 'Is it morning already?'

'Almost,' replied Fridolin. 'It's past four. I've just got home.' She didn't say anything, so he continued, 'The Court Counsellor is dead. He was dying when I got there . . . and of course I couldn't . . . leave the relatives alone at once.'

She nodded, yet hardly seemed to have heard or understood as she stared through him vacantly. He couldn't help feeling – irrational though the notion seemed to him at once – that she must be aware of what he had been through during the night. He bent over her and stroked her forehead. She shuddered slightly.

'What's the matter?' he asked again.

She just shook her head slowly. He stroked her hair. 'Albertine, what's wrong with you?'

'I was dreaming,' she said distantly.

'What were you dreaming about?' he asked mildly.

'Ah, so many things. I can't quite remember.'

'Perhaps you might be able to.'

'It was all so confused – and besides, I'm tired. But you must be tired too?'

'Not in the least, Albertine, and I won't get much sleep now. You know how it is when I get home this late – in fact the sensible thing would be to settle down at my desk at once – it's precisely when it's early in the morning like this that –' He broke off. 'But are you sure you wouldn't like to tell me your dream instead?' He smiled a little awkwardly.

'You really should lie down and rest,' she replied. He hesitated a moment, then did as she wished and stretched out beside her. Yet he avoided touching her. As if there were a sword between us, he thought, remembering how he had made the same sort of half-facetious remark under similar circumstances once before.

They both lapsed into silence and lay there with eyes open, each sensing the other's closeness and remoteness. After a while he rested his head on his arm and gazed at her for some time, as if trying to see more than the mere outline of her face.

'Your dream!' he said again suddenly; and it was as though she had been awaiting this demand. She stretched out her hand towards him; he took it as he was accustomed to, playing with her slender fingers distractedly rather than with tenderness. And so she began.

'Do you remember the room in the little villa on the Wörthersee where I stayed with my parents the summer we became engaged?'

He nodded.

'Well, that's how my dream began, with me entering that room – I don't quite know where from – like an actress walking on to the stage. All I knew was that my parents were travelling and had left me by myself. This seemed strange because the next day was supposed to be our wedding-day. But the wedding-dress had not yet arrived. Or was I perhaps mistaken?

I opened the wardrobe to have a look, but in place of the wedding-dress a collection of other clothes was hanging there: resplendent oriental operatic costumes, actually. Which should I wear as a wedding-dress? I wondered. Then suddenly the wardrobe closed or disappeared, I don't remember which. The room was brightly lit, but outside the window it was darkest night . . . All of a sudden you were standing out there; galley-slaves had rowed you, since I could just see them disappearing in the darkness. You were very richly dressed in gold and silk and had a dagger with a silver tassel at your side, and you lifted me out through the window. I too was now splendidly attired, like a princess, and we both stood there under the dawning sky, and a fine grey mist arose about our ankles. It was the district we were so familiar with: there before us lay the lake and mountain scenery, and I could also see the rustic houses like something from a toy-box. We two, however, were hovering, or rather flying above the mist, and I thought to myself: so this must be our honeymoon trip. Soon we were no longer flying but walking up a forest path, the one leading to the look-out, and suddenly we found ourselves high up in the mountains in a sort of clearing, which was fringed on three sides by woods, while towering up behind was a sheer wall of rock. Above us the starry sky was far bluer and more expansive than in the real world, and formed the ceiling to our bridal-chamber. Lovingly and tenderly, you took me in your arms.'

'I hope you loved me just as much,' remarked Fridolin, smiling wryly to himself.

'Even more so, I suspect,' Albertine replied seriously. 'And yet, how should I put it – despite our intimate embrace our love was tinged with sadness, as if by a presentiment of suffering to come. All of a sudden it was morning. The meadow was radiant and gaily coloured, the surrounding forest exquisitely bedewed, and sunlight played over the surface of the rock. And we too now felt that it was high time to rejoin the world of everyday society. But now something terrible occurred. Our clothes had disappeared. I was overcome by absolute horror, burning, all-consuming shame, and at the same time anger against you, as though you alone were responsible for this misfortune; and all this horror, shame and anger were infinitely more intense than anything I had ever experienced while awake. You, however, fully conscious of your guilt, fled down the mountain naked as you were to find some clothes for us. Once you had disappeared I felt totally at ease. I was neither sorry for you nor worried about you, but simply glad to be alone, and I ran happily across the meadow singing: it was a tune from a dance we had listened to at the masked ball. My voice sounded absolutely wonderful, and I wished that people could hear me far down in the city. I could not see this city, but I somehow knew what it was like. It lay there far below me and was surrounded by a high wall, an utterly fantastic city hard to describe in words. Not exactly oriental, nor medieval, but rather first one and then the other, at all events a city that long ago had disappeared for ever. But suddenly I was lying stretched out on the meadow in the sunshine, appearing much more beautiful than in real life, and as I lay there a gentleman stepped out of the forest, a young man in a light fashionable suit, looking, I now realize, very like the Dane I told you about yesterday. He continued on, greeting me politely as he passed, but not paying any particular attention to me, and walked straight towards the cliff, which he started to scrutinize, as though considering how it might be scaled. At the same time I could see you as well. You were down in the lost city, hurrying from house to house, from shop to shop beneath leafy arcades, then through a sort of Turkish bazaar, buying the most gorgeous things that you could find for me: clothes, linen, shoes and jewellery; and all of this you put into a yellow leather case which seemed to have room for everything. The whole time, though, you were pursued by a motley crowd of people – I couldn't see them, I could only hear their muffled threatening cries. And then the other man appeared again, the Dane who had stopped at the cliff face before. Again he came towards me from the forest – and I somehow knew that in the interim he had been right around the world. He looked quite different from before, yet was clearly the same person. As on the first occasion he stopped before the cliff, disappeared, then re-emerged out of the forest, disappeared again, and again came back out of the forest; this was repeated two, three or perhaps a hundred times. It was always the same person, yet always someone different, and he always greeted me as he came past, until finally he stopped short before me and looked searchingly at me. I laughed seductively, more so than ever in my life before, but when he stretched out his arms towards me I wanted to fly, yet failed to do so – and he lay down with me upon the meadow.'

She paused. Fridolin's throat was dry, and in the darkness of the room he noticed that Albertine was hiding her face in her hands.

'A curious dream,' he said. 'Is that how it ended?' And when she said no, 'Well then, continue.'

'It's not that easy,' she began again. 'It's almost impossible to express these things in words. Well – to me it was as through I had lived through innumerable days and nights, as though time and place no longer existed, and instead of the peaceful clearing surrounded by the woods and rock where I had been before there was now an extensive flowery plain stretching in every direction as far as the horizon. I had long since – how strange such temporal notions seem! – ceased to be alone in the meadow with that man. But whether there were three or ten or a thousand couples there beside myself, whether I could see them, and whether I gave myself to that man only or to others as well, I couldn't say. But just as that earlier feeling of horror and shame transcended anything conceivable in a wakeful state, it would be equally hard to conceive of anything in normal conscious life that could equal the freedom, the abandon, the sheer bliss I experienced in that dream. And yet throughout all this I never for a moment ceased to be aware of you. Yes, I could see you being seized, I think by soldiers, though there were clerics too among them, and I somehow knew that you were to be executed. I knew this without pity, without horror, with complete detachment. They led you out into a sort of castle courtyard. There you stood, your hands tied behind your back and naked. And just as I could see you even though elsewhere, you too could see me together with the man who held me in his arms, and all the other couples in that unending tide of nakedness which surged around me, in which I and the man embracing me represented but a single wave. While you were standing in the courtyard, a young woman wearing a diadem and purple gown appeared at a high arched window between red curtains. It was the princess of the land. She gazed down at you with a severe, questioning look. You stood alone while all the others remained aloof, pressed against the walls, and I could hear an ominous, spiteful mumbling and whispering. Then the princess leaned over the parapet. All became quiet and the princess made a sign, bidding you come up to her, and I knew she had decided to pardon you. But you didn't notice her, or didn't want to notice. Suddenly, still with your hands tied but wrapped in a black cloak, you were standing opposite her, not in her chamber but somehow hovering in mid-air. She was holding a sheet of parchment in her hand – your death sentence, in which your guilt and the reasons for your execution were recorded. She asked you – I could not hear her words and yet I knew – if you were prepared to become her paramour, in which case your death sentence could be remitted. You shook your head as a sign that you refused. I wasn't surprised, since all was preordained and the only possible outcome was that, whatever the danger, you would remain true to me unto all eternity. At this the princess shrugged her shoulders and waved into the void, whereupon you suddenly found yourself in an underground vault being chastised with whips, though I was unable to make out the people who were wielding them. The blood flowed from you in streams, and, seeing it flow, I was aware of my own horror without being surprised by it. Then the princess came up to you. Her hair was unbound and cascaded down her naked body as she held out the diadem towards you with both hands – and I knew she was the girl you had seen one morning naked on the gangplank of a bathing hut, on the beach in Denmark. She didn't say a word, but the unspoken implication of her presence, of her silence even, was whether you were willing to become her husband and so prince of the land. When you again declined, she vanished, but I could see at once that they were erecting a cross for you; not in the courtyard below but on the boundless flowery meadow, where I sat reclining in the arms of my lover among all the other couples. I could see you wandering alone and unguarded through old-fashioned streets, and yet I knew that your path was preordained and any escape impossible. Now you were coming up the forest path. I awaited you expectantly but without any overwhelming sympathy. Your body was covered with welts, though they were no longer bleeding. As you climbed higher and higher, the path became broader and the forest fell away on either side, until there you stood at the edge of the meadow, still an incredibly vast distance away. Yet you greeted me with smiling eyes, as if to indicate that you had carried out my wishes and were bringing all I needed: clothes and shoes and jewellery. But I found your conduct utterly ludicrous and pointless, and felt tempted to laugh in your face with scorn – all because, out of fidelity to me, you had turned down the hand of the princess, submitted to torture, and were now staggering up here to undergo a gruesome death. I ran towards you, and you too quickened your pace – I began to levitate and you also started floating through the air; but then suddenly we lost each other and I realized that we had simply flown past one another. I wanted you at least to hear my laughter while they nailed you to the cross. And so I burst out laughing as loudly and piercingly as I was able. That was the laughter, Fridolin – with which I awoke.'

She fell silent and remained completely still. He too did not move or say a word. At that moment anything would have sounded flat, mendacious and cowardly. The further she had progressed with her narrative, the more ridiculous and insignificant his own adventures so far seemed to him, and he swore to pursue them to the end and to report them faithfully to her, and so get even with this woman who had revealed herself through her dream for what she really was, faithless, cruel and treacherous, and whom at that moment he thought he hated more profoundly than he had ever loved her.

He now noticed that he was still holding her fingers in his hand and that, despite his determination to hate this woman, he felt an undiminished though more painful affection for those cool slender fingers that he knew so well; and involuntarily, indeed positively against his will, he softly pressed his lips to her hand before relinquishing it . . .

Albertine did not open her eyes, and Fridolin thought he could see her mouth, her brow, her whole countenance smiling with a joyous, transfigured, innocent expression, and he felt an impulse he himself did not understand, to bend over her and kiss her pallid forehead. But he restrained himself, recognizing that it was only the very understandable fatigue, after the exciting events of the last few hours, that had assumed the guise of sentimental tenderness.

But however matters stood with him at present, whatever decisions he might reach in the next few hours, what he urgently needed at that moment was to escape, at least for a while, into sleep and oblivion.

On the night following his mother's death he had been able to fall into a deep and dreamless sleep, and should he not succeed in doing so tonight? So he stretched out beside Albertine, who by now appeared to have gone to sleep. As if there were a sword between us, he thought again. And then: we are lying here side by side like mortal enemies.

VI

He was woken at seven o'clock that morning by the gentle knocking of the maid. He cast a quick glance at Albertine. Sometimes, though not always, this knocking would wake her too. Today she slept on tranquilly, all too tranquilly: Fridolin hurriedly got ready. He wanted to see his little daughter before leaving. She was lying peacefully in her white bed, her hands curled into little fists, the way children do. He kissed her forehead. And once again he tiptoed to the door of the bedroom where Albertine was still lying motionless. Then he left, the monk's habit and pilgrim's hat stowed safely in his doctor's bag. He had worked out his programme for the day carefully and even with a touch of pedantry. First on his list was a visit to a lawyer quite close by who was seriously ill. Fridolin examined him thoroughly, found his condition somewhat improved, expressed his satisfaction with genuine pleasure and prescribed a well-tried remedy with the usual admonitions. Then he went directly to the cavernous basement tavern where Nachtigall had played the piano the previous evening. That establishment was still closed, but in the coffee-house upstairs the lady at the till happened to know that Nachtigall boarded at a small hotel in Leopoldstadt. A quarter of an hour later Fridolin drew up in front of it. It was a squalid little boarding-house. The lobby smelled of unaired beds, bad fat and chicory coffee. An evil-looking porter with piercing red-rimmed eyes, well accustomed to police interrogations, was willing to furnish him with information. Herr Nachtigall had driven up at five that morning in the company of two gentlemen who, perhaps deliberately, had made sure they would be virtually unrecognizable by wearing scarves over their faces. While Nachtigall had gone up to his room, these gentlemen had paid his rent for the previous four weeks; and when after half an hour he had still not reappeared, one of them had fetched him down, whereupon all three had driven to the Northern District Station. Nachtigall had appeared to be extremely agitated; indeed, why should one not tell the whole truth to a gentleman who inspired such confidence – he had tried to slip a note to the porter, but the two gentlemen had intervened at once. Any letters for Herr Nachtigall, the two gentlemen had explained, would be collected by someone authorized to do so. Fridolin took his leave, thankful that he had his doctor's bag with him as he came out of the main door: that way people would not take him for a lodger but for someone there officially. From Nachtigall, then, there was nothing to be gleaned. They had been very careful, and evidently had every reason for being so.

Next he drove to the costumier's establishment. Herr Gibiser opened the door himself. 'I'm returning the costume I rented,' said Fridolin, 'and would like to pay you whatever is owing.' Herr Gibiser named a modest sum, accepted the money, made an entry in a hefty ledger, and looked up somewhat puzzled from his desk, as Fridolin made no sign of leaving.

'I'm here, furthermore,' said Fridolin in the tone of a prosecuting lawyer, 'to have a word with you about your daughter.'

Herr Gibiser's nostrils quivered faintly, whether with uneasiness, mockery or irritation was difficult to tell.

'What do you mean, sir?' he asked in a tone which was equally hard to interpret.

'Yesterday you mentioned,' said Fridolin, one hand resting on the desk with fingers splayed, 'that your daughter was not quite normal mentally. The circumstances in which we encountered her actually made this quite clear. And, as chance made me a participant, or at least a witness, to that extraordinary little scene, I wanted to urge you, Herr Gibiser, to consult a doctor.'

Gibiser, twirling an unnaturally long feather quill in his hand, considered Fridolin with an insolent look.

'And might you, sir, be so obliging as to take on her treatment?'

'I would ask you,' replied Fridolin sharply but also a little hoarsely, 'not to put words into my mouth.'

At that moment the door leading to the inner rooms was opened and a young gentleman, his coat open over his evening suit, came out. Fridolin knew at once that it could be none other than one of the vehmic court judges from the previous night, and that he was coming from the Pierrette's room. He seemed put out when he caught sight of Fridolin, but controlled himself as he greeted Gibiser with a quick wave of the hand, then lit a cigarette with the lighter on the desk and left the apartment.

'I see,' remarked Fridolin with a sneer of contempt and a bitter taste in his mouth.

'How do you mean, sir?' asked Gibiser, completely unruffled.

'So you decided, Herr Gibiser,' he said, gazing meaningfully from the apartment door to the one from which the judge had just emerged, 'to dispense with informing the police.'

'We have come to a different understanding, doctor,' said Gibiser coolly and stood up, as if an audience had been concluded. As Fridolin turned to go, Gibiser opened the door solicitously and said with an impassive face, 'If you should need anything again, sir . . . it wouldn't have to be specifically a monk's habit.'

Fridolin slammed the door behind him. Well, that's seen to, he thought, with a feeling of exasperation that even to him seemed out of all proportion. He hurried down the stairs, made for the polyclinic without undue haste, and telephoned home at once to inquire whether any of his patients had sent for him, whether the post had come, and whether there was any other news. The maid had scarcely finished answering when Albertine herself came to the phone and greeted him. She repeated everything the maid had just said, and without any awkwardness told him she had just got up and was about to have breakfast with the child.

'Give her a kiss from me,' said Fridolin, 'and enjoy your meal.'

Her voice had done him good, and precisely for that reason he rang off almost at once. He had wanted to ask what Albertine's plans were for the morning, but what business of his was that? In the depths of his soul he had after all already done with her, however life might go on outwardly. The blonde nurse helped him out of his coat and handed him his white doctor's tunic. As she did so, she smiled at him a little, as she tended to smile at everyone, whether they were interested in her or not.

A few minutes later he was on the ward. The head physician had left word that he had been suddenly called away for a consultation, and his colleagues were to do the rounds without him. Fridolin felt almost happy as he went from bed to bed followed by the students, examining patients, writing prescriptions and consulting professionally with registrars and nurses. There were all sorts of new developments. The locksmith Karl Rödel had died during the night. The post-mortem was at five that afternoon. In the women's ward a bed had become vacant, but had already been filled. The woman from bed no. 17 had had to be transferred for surgery. Now and then questions to do with personnel were touched on too. The new director of the clinic was to be appointed the day after tomorrow; Hügelmann, who was currently a professor at Marburg and four years ago had still only been Stellwag's second assistant, had the best chance. A rapid career, thought Fridolin. I shall never be considered for the headship of a department, because I don't have my dissertation in hand. Too late. But how so? One would have to start doing research again, or pick up work already embarked on much more seriously. Private practice did still leave one enough free time.

He asked Dr Fuchstaler to take charge of the rounds, though he had to admit that he would rather have stayed on than drive out to the Galitzinberg. And yet it had to be done. He did not just owe it to himself to pursue the matter further; and there were many things still to be attended to today. And so, just in case, he decided to entrust Dr Fuchstaler with the evening rounds as well. The young girl with suspected acute bronchitis over in the last bed smiled at him. She was the one who during a recent examination had taken the opportunity to press her breast so intimately against his cheek. Fridolin returned her gaze ungraciously and turned away with a frown. They're all the same, he thought bitterly, and Albertine no different from the rest – in fact she's the worst of them all. We'll have to part. Things can never be the same again between us.

On the stairs he exchanged a few words with a colleague from the surgical department. Well, how was the woman who had been transferred to them last night coming along? Personally, he didn't see the need to operate. Would they forward the results of the histology tests to him?

'You may depend upon it, my dear colleague.'

At the corner he took a cab. He consulted his notebook – an absurd little charade for the coachman's benefit – as though he were just making up his mind. 'Ottakring,' he said finally, 'take the road up the Galitzinberg. I'll tell you where to stop.'

In the cab he was suddenly overwhelmed by an ardent yet anguished feeling, indeed almost a sense of guilt, at having all but forgotten his beautiful saviour during the last few hours. Would he be able to find the house again? It shouldn't be all that difficult. The question was: what then? Notify the police? That could have dangerous consequences for the woman who perhaps had sacrificed herself, or been prepared to sacrifice herself for him. Or should he engage a private detective? That seemed rather sordid and not quite worthy of him. But what else could he do? He had neither the time nor, probably, the talent to carry out the necessary investigations effectively himself. A secret society? Well, secret undoubtedly. But among themselves, were they personally acquainted? Aristocrats, even attached to the court? He thought of certain archdukes whom one could imagine capable of this kind of escapade. And the ladies? Probably . . . rounded up from various houses of ill-repute. Well, that was far from certain. High-class merchandise, at all events. But what about the woman who had sacrificed herself for him? Sacrificed? Why did he persist in imagining that it had really been a sacrifice! A charade. Quite obviously the whole thing had been a charade. Actually, he should be glad that he had got out of it so lightly. At least he had preserved his dignity. The courtiers must certainly have noticed that he was no greenhorn. She at all events had noticed it. Very probably she preferred him to all those archdukes or whatever they had been.

At the end of the Liebhart Valley, where the road begins to climb more steeply, he got out, dismissing the cab as a precaution. The pale blue sky was flecked with little white clouds, and the sun was shining with the warmth of spring. He looked back, but could see nothing to arouse suspicion. No cab, no one on foot. Slowly he walked up the hill. His coat began to feel heavy; he took it off and threw it over his shoulder. He reached the spot where he had to turn right into the side-road leading to the mysterious house; he couldn't go wrong; the road descended, but not as steeply as he had imagined when being driven down during the night. A quiet road. In one front garden there were rose-bushes wrapped carefully in straw, while in the next there was a small pram; a little boy clad in blue woollen clothes was tottering to and fro; from a ground-floor window a young woman watched him with a smile. Then came a vacant plot, then a fenced-off garden run to seed, then a small villa, then a stretch of lawn and here, there could be no mistake – here was the house that he was looking for. It didn't look particularly large or grand, being a modest, single-storey Empire-style villa which had evidently been renovated not too long ago. The green shutters were all let down, and there was nothing to indicate that it was inhabited. Fridolin looked all around. There was no one about in the street, apart from two boys further down who were walking away from him with books under their arms. He stood outside the garden gate. What next? Should he simply walk away? That seemed too ridiculous. He looked round for the bell. And suppose they were to open the door, what should he say? Simply inquire, perhaps, whether this fine country residence might be available for rent over the summer? But the front door had already opened and an old servant in simple morning livery came out and walked slowly down the narrow path towards the garden gate. He was holding a letter which he silently handed through the bars to Fridolin, whose heart was pounding.

'For me?' he asked hesitantly. The servant nodded,

turned and withdrew, and the front door closed behind him. What can this mean? Fridolin asked himself. Perhaps it's from her? Perhaps *she* is the one who owns the house? He walked quickly back up the street and only then noticed that his name was written on the envelope in imperious Gothic lettering. At the corner he opened the letter, unfolded the sheet and read, 'Give up your investigations, which are completely futile, and consider this a second warning. We hope, for your sake, that a further one will not be necessary.' He let the note fall to his side.

This message disappointed him in every way; but at least it was quite different from what he had foolishly imagined. Certainly its tone was rather more restrained than cutting. And it suggested that the people who had sent it did not feel at all secure.

A second warning? Why? Ah, yes, the first had been the one issued to him the previous night. But why a second – and not a final warning? Did they want to try his courage yet again? Did he have to pass some sort of test? And how did they know his name? There was nothing strange about that, they had probably forced Nachtigall to reveal it. And besides – he smiled at his own forgetfulness – his monogram and full address were sewn into the lining of his coat.

Yet even if he had progressed no further than before, on the whole the letter had been reassuring – although quite why this should be so he couldn't say. To be more precise, he was convinced that the woman for whose fate he had feared was still alive, and that he alone could find her if he proceeded with cunning and circumspection.

When he reached home a little tired, yet in a strange mood of release which at the same time he felt to be deceptive, Albertine and the child had already had their lunch, but kept him company while he ate his meal. There, sitting opposite him, was the woman who last night would have calmly had him crucified, now looking angelic, domesticated and maternal, and to his surprise he felt no hatred for her whatsoever. Savouring his food, he found himself in an excitable but also more light-hearted mood and, as was his wont, talked animatedly about the day's little professional incidents, dwelling particularly on matters to do with medical personnel, which he was accustomed to relay to Albertine in detail. He explained that the nomination of Hügelmann was as good as certain, and mentioned his own resolve to resume research more vigorously. Albertine was familiar with these moods, and knew that they tended not to last that long, and a smile betrayed her scepticism. Fridolin became more enthusiastic, and Albertine gently stroked his hair to soothe him. He winced slightly and turned towards the child, thus evading further painful contact. He lifted the child on to his lap, and was beginning to rock her on his knees when the maid announced that several patients were already waiting. As if released, Fridolin stood up and, observing casually that Albertine and the child ought to take advantage of the beautiful sunny afternoon and go out for a walk, entered his consulting-room.

In the course of the next two hours Fridolin had six regular patients and two new ones to attend to. During each appointment he was in excellent form, examining his patients, making notes, prescribing – and was pleased to find himself feeling so wonderfully fresh and clearheaded after two nights spent almost entirely without sleep.

When he had finished his consulting, as usual he looked in again on his wife and child, and was pleased to see that Albertine's mother had dropped by for a visit, and that the child was having a lesson with her French teacher. And it was not until he reached the stairs that he again had the sense that all this order, balance and security in his life were really an illusion and a lie.

Even though he had excused himself from the afternoon rounds, he found himself irresistibly drawn to the clinic. There were two cases that were particularly relevant to his more immediate research plans, and for a while he occupied himself with them more intensively than he had previously done. Then he had one more call to attend to in the centre of town, so that by the time he found himself outside the old house in the Schreyvogelgasse it was already seven in the evening. Only then, as he looked up at Marianne's window, did her image, which had faded more than that of all the others in the interim, come to life again. Here at least he would not go unrequited. Here he could begin his work of vengeance without too much trouble; here there were no difficulties and no danger; and the betrayal of a bridegroom which might have given others pause was for him merely an additional inducement. Indeed, the idea of betrayal, lying, infidelity and a bit of hanky-panky here and there, all under the noses of Marianne, Albertine, the good Dr Roediger, all the world – the thought of leading a kind of double life, of being at once a hard-working reliable progressive doctor, a decent husband, family man and father, and at the same time a profligate, seducer and cynic who played with men and women as his whim dictated – this prospect seemed to him at that moment peculiarly agreeable. And the most agreeable thing of all about it was that later on, when Albertine imagined herself secure in the haven of her tranquil conjugal and family life, he would be able to smile coldly and confess his sins to her, and thus get even for all the bitterness and shame she had brought upon him in her dream.

In the entrance hall he found himself face to face with Dr Roediger, who held out his hand to him with unsuspecting cordiality.

'How is Marianne?' asked Fridolin. 'Has she calmed down a little?'

Roediger shrugged his shoulders. 'She's been expecting the end long enough, doctor. It was only when they collected the body around noon today—'

'Ah, so that's already taken place?'

Roediger nodded. 'The funeral is at three o'clock tomorrow afternoon.'

Fridolin looked straight ahead. 'The relatives – are they still with Marianne?'

'No,' replied Roediger, 'she's alone at present. I'm sure she'll be pleased to see you again. Tomorrow my mother and I are taking her to Mödling,' and in response to Fridolin's polite look of inquiry, 'You see, my parents have a little house there. Goodbye, doctor. I still have several matters to attend to. The things that have to be seen to in a – case like this! I hope I shall see you upstairs when I get back.' And he stepped out of the door into the street.

Fridolin hesitated a moment, then slowly climbed the stairs. He rang and Marianne herself opened the door. She was dressed in black and had a black necklace made of jet around her neck, which he had never seen her wear before. Her face gradually turned red.

'You've taken your time coming,' she said with a wan smile.

'My apologies, Marianne, but it's been an unusually busy day.'

He followed her through to the dead man's room, where the bed now stood empty, and into the adjacent room, where yesterday he had made out the Court Counsellor's death certificate beneath the picture of the officer in the white uniform. A little lamp was still burning on the desk, so that a dim light suffused the room. Marianne bade him take a seat on the black leather divan, while she herself sat down at the desk opposite.

'I just met Dr Roediger in the hall. So you're off to the country tomorrow already?'

Marianne looked at him as though surprised at the cool tone of his question, and her shoulders drooped as he continued in a voice that sounded almost harsh, 'I think that's very sensible.' And he went on soberly to explain how beneficial the effects of good air and a change of scene would be.

She sat there without moving and tears flowed down her cheeks. He observed this without the slightest compassion, indeed with impatience, and was filled with alarm at the thought that any minute she might perhaps again prostrate herself at his feet and renew her declaration of the day before. She said nothing, so he got up briskly. 'I'm very sorry, Marianne, but –' and he looked at his watch.

She raised her head, looked at Fridolin, and her

tears continued to flow. He would have liked to offer a few words of comfort, but couldn't bring himself to do so.

'I imagine you'll be spending several days in the country,' he began awkwardly. 'I do hope you'll let me know how you . . . Dr Roediger tells me that your wedding is to be quite soon, by the way. Allow me to congratulate you both.'

She did not stir, as though she had not registered his congratulations or his farewell. He held out his hand, but she didn't take it, and in a tone almost of reproach he repeated, 'Well, I sincerely hope you'll let me know how you're getting on. Goodbye, Marianne.' She just sat there as if turned to stone. He began to leave, pausing at the door for a second as if to give her one last chance to call him back, but she seemed instead to have turned her head away, and so he closed the door behind him. Outside in the passage he felt something bordering on remorse. For a moment he considered turning back, but felt that that would have been even more ridiculous.

But what now? Home again? What else! After all, he couldn't embark on anything more today. What about tomorrow? And how should he set about things? He felt helpless and inept, and everything seemed to be slipping from his grasp; everything was becoming increasingly unreal, even his home, his wife, his child, his profession, his very identity, as he trudged on mechanically through the evening streets, turning things over in his mind.

The town hall clock struck half past seven. But it really didn't matter how late it was: time seemed to stretch out before him in utter superfluity. No one and nothing concerned him any longer. He felt full of self-pity. Fleetingly, and without any serious intent, he thought of driving to some station, taking a train to wherever it might be and vanishing from the lives of everyone who knew him, to resurface somewhere overseas and begin a new life as someone else. He remembered a number of remarkable cases of double identity he knew about from books on psychiatry: a person would disappear suddenly from a perfectly orderly milieu, be forgotten and then return months or years later, unable to remember where he had been for all that time; afterwards someone who had known him in some distant land would recognize him, yet the home-comer would know nothing about it whatsoever. True, such things happened very rarely, but they had been authenticated none the less. And in a milder form they were experienced by a great many people. What about when one awoke from dreams, for example? Of course, there one could remember . . . But there were also surly dreams which one forgot completely, of which nothing remained but some mysterious aura, some obscure bemusement. Or else one remembered later, much later, and could no longer tell whether one had experienced something or merely dreamed it. Except that –!

And as he wandered on, unconsciously heading in the direction of his apartment, he found himself not far from the dark, rather disreputable street where less than twenty-four hours ago he had followed that abandoned creature to her tawdry yet comfortable lodgings. But why should she particularly be thought of as *abandoned*? Or this particular street be called *disreputable*? Curious how, seduced by words, again and again one labels and condemns people, destinies and streets through sheer idle force of habit. Hadn't that young girl been the most charming and even the purest of all those with whom the strange circumstances of the previous evening had brought him into contact? He felt himself becoming a little aroused as

he thought of her. Then he also recollected his inten-
tions on the previous day and, quickly making up his
mind, went into the next shop to purchase various
dainty things to eat. He continued on close to the
walls of the houses with his little parcel, feeling
almost happy at the thought that he was about to do
something sensible and even perhaps praiseworthy.
Despite this, however, he turned up his collar as he
stepped into the entrance hall and ran up the stairs
several steps at a time. The apartment doorbell
resounded in his ears with an unpleasant shrillness,
and when he was informed by an evil-looking woman
that Mizzi was not at home, he breathed a sigh of
relief. But before the woman had a chance to accept
the package for the absent girl, another youngish,
not unattractive woman wrapped in a sort of dressing-
gown came out into the hall and said, 'Who're you
looking for, sir? Mizzi? She won't be back in a hurry.'

The old woman signalled to her to be quiet; but
Fridolin, eager to receive confirmation of what he
had somehow already guessed, simply said, 'She's in
hospital, isn't she?'

'Well, if you already know, sir! But I'm quite
healthy, thank God,' she protested gaily and came

up close to Fridolin with half-open lips, thrusting her opulent body back cheekily, so that her dressing-gown fell open. 'I just came up as I was passing to give something to Mizzi,' said Fridolin evasively, and suddenly he felt like a schoolboy. Then, in an altered, matter-of-fact tone, he asked, 'Which clinic is she in?'

The young woman mentioned that of a professor under whom Fridolin had studied several years ago. Then she added good-naturedly, 'Let me have the little parcel, I'll bring it her tomorrow. You can trust me not to nibble. And I'll be sure to send your greetings and to tell her you've been true to her.'

At the same time she moved closer and smiled at him. But when he drew back a little, she gave up the idea at once and remarked consolingly, 'The doctor said she should be home again in six weeks or eight at the latest!'

When Fridolin stepped out of the main door into the street, he felt tears welling up in his throat; yet he was well aware that this was not so much an indication that he had been moved as a sign of incipient nervous collapse. He deliberately started off at a brisker and more vigorous pace than was appropriate to his state of mind. Was this latest experience to be taken as a further, or a final, indication that all his efforts were doomed to failure? But how so? His escape from such a serious danger could equally well be taken as a good omen. And wasn't avoiding danger precisely what everything depended on? Many more perils were bound to lie ahead. And he had no intention of abandoning his inquiry after the beautiful woman of the previous night. Admittedly time was now running out. And besides, the manner in which this inquiry was to be conducted had to be considered carefully. If only there were someone he could consult! But he did not know anyone he would have been willing to confide in about last night's adventures. For years he had not been on intimate terms with anyone except his wife, and he could hardly consult her on this matter – neither this nor any other matter. For whichever way one wished to look at it, last night she had had him crucified.

And now he understood why instead of taking him home his steps unconsciously kept leading him in the opposite direction. He simply could not yet face Albertine. The most sensible thing was to have his evening meal out somewhere, then see to his two patients at the hospital – and under no circumstances go home – 'home!' – before he could be certain that Albertine would already be asleep.

He entered a coffee-house, one of the quieter, more formal ones near the town hall, telephoned to say that they should not expect him home for supper, hastily rang off lest Albertine should come to the phone, and then took a window seat and drew the curtain. A gentleman inconspicuously dressed in a dark overcoat sat down in a remote corner of the room. Fridolin remembered having seen his features somewhere before during the day. That could of course have been mere coincidence. He picked up an evening paper and read a few lines here and there, as he had done the previous evening in another coffee-house: reports on political events, the theatre, art, literature and all sorts of misadventures, large and small. In some town in America he had never heard of a theatre had burned down. Peter Korand, a master sweep, had thrown himself out of a window. To Fridolin it somehow seemed odd that even chimney-sweeps should commit suicide occasionally, and he couldn't help asking himself whether the man had had a proper wash beforehand, or simply plunged into oblivion all blackened as he was. In a fashionable hotel in the centre of the city a woman had taken poison: a lady who had checked in there a few days before under the name of Baroness D., a lady of quite remarkable beauty ... Well there were so many remarkably beautiful young ladies ... There was no reason to assume that Baroness D., or rather the lady who had checked in to the hotel under the name of Baroness D., and the person he was thinking of were one and the same. And yet – his heart was pounding and the paper trembling in his hand. In a fashionable hotel in the centre ... which one? Why so mysterious? So discreet?

He put the paper down and noticed that the gentleman over in the far corner quickly thrust a large illustrated newspaper in front of his face like a screen. Immediately Fridolin too picked up his paper again, and in that instant he knew for certain that Baroness D. could be none other than the woman of the previous night ... In a fashionable hotel in the centre of town ... There weren't all that many that would have been considered acceptable – by a Baroness D. And now, come what may, this lead had to be followed up. He summoned the waiter, paid and left. At the door he turned again towards the suspicious gentleman in the corner. But strangely enough he had already disappeared.

A serious case of poisoning. But she was alive . . . At the time they had discovered her, she was still alive. And, after all, there was no reason to assume that they had not rescued her in time. In any event, dead or alive, he was going to find her. He was going to see her – come hell or high water – whether she were alive or dead. He simply had to see her; nobody on earth could prevent him seeing the woman who had gone to her death for his sake, indeed *in place of him!* He was to blame for her death – he alone – if she indeed it was. Yes, it was her without a doubt. She had come home at four in the morning in the company of two gentlemen. Probably the same two who had escorted Nachtigall to the station a few hours later. They could scarcely have a very clear conscience, either of them.

He stood in the broad open square in front of the town hall and looked around. There were only a few people in sight, and the suspicious gentleman from the coffee-house was not among them. And what if he were – these men were clearly frightened, and he was more than a match for them. Fridolin hurried on and took a cab from the Ringstrasse, driving first to the Hotel Bristol. There, as if authorized or commissioned to inquire, he asked the porter whether Baroness D., who was said to have poisoned herself that morning, had been staying at this hotel. The porter did not seem especially surprised, perhaps because he took Fridolin to be someone from the police or some official; and he politely replied that the unfortunate event had not occurred here but at the Hotel Archduke Karl.

Fridolin drove at once to the hotel in question, and there received the news that Baroness D. had been rushed to the General Hospital as soon as she had been discovered. Fridolin asked how the suicide attempt had come to light. What had caused them to become concerned at noon about a lady who had not arrived home until four that morning? That was simple enough: two gentlemen (again two gentlemen!) had asked for her at about eleven o'clock. As the lady had not responded to repeated telephone calls, the chambermaid had knocked on her door; since there was still no response and the door was locked from within, they had had no choice but to break it open, and had found the Baroness lying in bed unconscious.

'And the two gentlemen?' asked Fridolin, feeling like someone from the secret police.

Well, yes, one couldn't help wondering about the two gentlemen, since while all this was going on they had disappeared without a trace. Furthermore, they had not apparently been dealing with a real Baroness Dubieski, the name under which the lady had registered at the hotel. This was the first time she had ever stayed at that hotel, and at least among the aristocracy there was no family of that name.

Fridolin thanked him for the information, and, as one of the hotel managers who had just come up was beginning to look at him with disconcerting curiosity, he withdrew in some haste, got back into his cab and drove over to the hospital. At the reception desk a few minutes later, he not only learned that the so-called Baroness Dubieski had been delivered to the second in-patients' clinic, but that despite the best efforts of the doctors she had died at five that afternoon without regaining consciousness.

Fridolin heaved a sigh of relief, or so he imagined, but it was a heavy sigh that escaped him for all that. The official on duty looked up at him in some surprise. Fridolin pulled himself together at once, took leave of him politely and a minute later was standing in the open air. The hospital garden was almost deserted. In an avenue close by a nurse in a white bonnet and blue and white striped smock was just walking past under a street lamp. 'Dead,' said Fridolin aloud to himself. – If it's her. What if it isn't? And if she's still alive, how am I to find her?

The question of where the body of the unknown woman was at that moment could be answered readily enough. As she had only died a few hours ago, she would still be in the mortuary, only a few hundred yards from there. And for him, as a doctor of course, there would be no difficulty about gaining admission, even at that late hour. And yet – what did he hope to achieve there? He had seen only her body, never her face, except fleetingly last night as he had left the dance-hall or, more accurately, been expelled from it. He had not taken this factor into consideration before, because ever since he had first read the notice in the paper he had been imagining the faceless suicidal woman as having Albertine's features; indeed, as he now realized with a shudder, his wife had been incessantly hovering before his eyes as the woman he was seeking. And again he asked himself what he really hoped to find in the mortuary. Were he to have discovered her alive again, today, tomorrow – years hence, no matter when, where or under what circumstances, he was utterly convinced that he would have recognized her at once from her walk, her bearing and above all her voice. As it was, however, all he would be seeing again was her body, a dead female body – a face he was unfamiliar with except for the eyes – eyes which were now extinguished. Yes – he knew those eyes and that hair too, which at the very last minute before they dragged him from the room had been let down to cover her nakedness. Would that be enough for him to tell, without the shadow of a doubt, whether or not it was she?

With slow, hesitant steps he made his way across the courtyards to the Pathology Institute. He found the main gate unlocked, so he did not have to ring. The stone floor echoed beneath his feet as he walked along the dimly lit passage. A familiar, almost domestic smell of various chemicals, which drowned out the native odour of the building, enveloped Fridolin. He knocked at the door of the histology lab, where he suspected there might be a technician still at work. On hearing a rather irritable 'Come in', he entered the high-ceilinged, almost festively illuminated room, in the middle of which, as Fridolin had half expected, his old fellow student, the Institute technician Dr Adler had just withdrawn his eye from a microscope, and was now rising from his chair.

'Ah, my dear colleague,' said Dr Adler, still a little reluctantly but also with surprise, 'to what do I owe the honour at such an unusual hour?'

'Sorry to disturb you,' said Fridolin. 'You're in the middle of something.'

'I am indeed,' replied Adler with an acerbity that had been characteristic of him even during their student days. Then he added in a lighter tone, 'What else would I be doing in these hallowed halls at midnight? But of course you're not disturbing me in the least. How can I be of service?'

And, as Fridolin did not reply at once, 'Addison, whom you sent down to us today, is still lying in untouched loveliness over there. Post-mortem tomorrow morning at eight thirty.' In response to Fridolin's gesture of demurral, he said, 'I see, then it's the lung tumour! Well, the histology test revealed an indisputable sarcoma. So no need to go grey over that one.'

Fridolin shook his head again. 'It's not a – professional matter.'

'So much the better,' said Adler. 'I was beginning to think a guilty conscience might be driving you down here at this ungodly hour.'

'In a way it does have to do with a guilty conscience, or rather with questions of conscience in general.'

'Oh!'

'Well, to put it bluntly' – he endeavoured to find an appropriately dry, innocuous tone – 'I wanted some information about a woman who died of morphine poisoning in the second clinic this evening and should by now have been laid out down here, supposedly a certain Baroness Dubieski.' He continued more quickly, 'You see, I suspect this Baroness Dubieski might be a person I knew briefly many years ago. And I'm curious to know whether my suspicion is correct.'

'*Suicidium?*' asked Adler.

Fridolin nodded. 'Yes, she killed herself,' he said, translating, as if by doing so he could reaffirm the private nature of the whole business.

Adler humorously pointed a finger at Fridolin. 'Out of unrequited love for your lordship?'

Fridolin protested a little irritably. 'This Baroness Dubieski's suicide had nothing whatsoever to do with me personally.'

'I beg your pardon, I've no wish to be indiscreet. We can go and check at once. To my knowledge, there have been no requests this evening from the forensic people. Well, anyway –'

A legal inquest flashed through Fridolin's mind. It might well come to that. Who knows whether her suicide was really deliberate? He again thought of the two gentlemen who had disappeared so suddenly from the hotel, after they had learned about the suicide attempt. The whole affair might still turn into a criminal case of the first order. And might not he, Fridolin, be summoned as a witness – indeed, wouldn't he be obliged to report to the law-court of his own free will?

He followed Adler across the hall to the door opposite, which stood ajar. The high, bare room was dimly illuminated by the low flame from a double gas lamp. Only a few of the dozen or so mortuary beds were occupied. A few corpses were lying there stark naked, the others were covered with linen sheets. Fridolin went up to the first table, next to the door, and carefully removed the sheet from the head of the deceased. Suddenly it was lit up by the harsh light from Adler's pocket torch. Fridolin saw a yellow, grey-bearded man's face and covered it with the shroud again at once. On the next table lay the thin naked body of a young man. Coming over from another table, Adler said, 'A woman in her sixties or seventies, that wouldn't be her.'

But Fridolin, as though suddenly and irresistibly drawn there, had moved over to the far end of the room, where he could just make out the pale corpse of a woman. The head was lying to one side; long dark strands of hair fell almost to the floor. Fridolin stretched out his hand to adjust the head, but then, with a revulsion normally quite alien to him as a doctor, he hesitated. Adler had come up and, gesturing towards those behind them, said, 'It can't be any of the others – what about her?' And he flashed his torch at the woman's head, which Fridolin, overcoming his aversion, had just taken in both hands and raised a little. An ashen face with half-closed lids stared back at him. The jaw hung open loosely, the thin, raised upper lip left the bluish gums and a row of white teeth exposed. Whether this face had ever been beautiful, whether yesterday it had still been so, Fridolin would not have cared to say: now it was a completely null, vacant face, the face of death. It could equally well have belonged to a woman of eighteen or thirty-eight.

'Is this her?' asked Adler.

Unconsciously Fridolin bent lower, as if the intensity of his gaze might wrest an answer from those rigid features. And yet at the same time he was conscious that even if it were *her* face, *her* eyes, the same eyes that yesterday had gazed into his ablaze with life, he could never know for certain – and perhaps didn't even want to know. Gently he laid the head back against the slab, and let his gaze follow the torch-light over the dead body. Was it her body? That wonderful, blooming body that yesterday had tortured him with longing? He looked at the yellowish, wrinkled neck, noticed the two small girlish, yet slightly sagging breasts, between which the breast-bone stood out under the pale skin with gruesome clarity, as if the process of decay already had set in; followed the contours of her lower body, noticing the way the well-formed thighs spread out impassively from shadowy regions that had lost their mystery and meaning; and observed the slight out-ward curve of the knees, the sharp outline of the shin bones and the slender feet with toes turned inwards. One after the other these features receded once more into the gloom, as the beam from the torch swiftly retraced its path, and, trembling slightly, came to rest on the face again. Almost as if driven by some unseen power, Fridolin touched the woman's brow, cheeks, arms and shoulders with both hands; then he inter-twined his fingers with the dead woman's as if to fondle them, and, stiff as they were, they seemed to be attempting to move and to take hold of his; indeed, he thought he could detect a faint and distant gleam in the eyes beneath those half-closed lids, trying to make contact with his own; and, as if drawn on by some enchantment, he bent down over her.

Then suddenly he heard a whisper close behind him: 'What on earth are you up to?'

Fridolin came abruptly to his senses. He let go the dead woman's fingers, took hold of her slender wrists and carefully, even a shade pedantically, placed her ice-cold arms beside her. He felt as though it were only now, at that very moment, that this woman had died. Then he turned round, found his way to the door and across the echoing passage, and re-entered the laboratory they had left earlier. Adler followed silently, locking the door behind him.

Fridolin went over to the washbasin. 'May I?' he said, and washed his hands thoroughly with soap and Lysol. Meanwhile Adler seemed eager to resume his interrupted work without delay. He had switched his light on again, adjusted the micrometer and was peering into the microscope. When Fridolin came over to take his leave, he was already engrossed in his work.

'Do you want to have a look at the culture?' he asked.

'What for?' asked Fridolin absently.

'Well, to satisfy your conscience,' replied Adler, as though he were taking it as understood that the purpose of Fridolin's visit had been medical and scientific.

'Can you interpret it?' he asked, while Fridolin looked into the microscope. 'It's a fairly recent colour-contrastive method.'

Fridolin nodded without removing his eye from the microscope. 'Perfect, really,' he remarked, 'a splendid colour picture, you might say.'

And he inquired about various details the new technique involved.

Adler gave him the information he required, and Fridolin remarked that the novel technique might well prove very useful in some work he was planning for the near future. He asked if he might come again tomorrow or the next day to seek further information.

'Always pleased to be of service,' said Adler, and accompanied Fridolin along the echoing flagstones to the main door, which meanwhile had been locked, and opened it with his own key.

'You are staying on?' asked Fridolin.

'But of course,' replied Adler, 'this is by far the best time to work – from about midnight until morning. At least I'm reasonably safe from interruptions.'

'Quite so,' said Fridolin with a quiet, slightly guilty smile.

Adler placed his hand reassuringly on Fridolin's arm, then asked with a certain diffidence, 'Well – was it her?'

Fridolin hesitated a moment, then nodded silently, and was scarcely conscious that this affirmation might quite possibly be untrue. For whether the woman now lying in the mortuary was the one whom twenty-four hours earlier he had held naked in his arms, to the wild accompaniment of Nachtigall's piano, or whether she was really a complete stranger, of one thing he was absolutely certain. Even if the woman he was looking for, had desired and for an hour perhaps loved were still alive, and regardless of how she continued to conduct her life, what lay behind him in that vaulted room – in the gloom of flickering gas lamps, a shadow among shades, as dark, meaningless and devoid of mystery as they – could now mean nothing to him but the pale corpse of the previous night, destined irrevocably for decay.

VII

He hurried home through the dark deserted streets, and a few minutes later, having undressed in his consulting-room as he had done twenty-four hours earlier, he entered the marital bedroom as quietly as possible.

He could hear Albertine's calm, regular breathing and see the outline of her head silhouetted against the soft pillow. A feeling of tenderness and of security he had not expected overwhelmed him. And he resolved to tell her the whole story quite soon, perhaps even tomorrow, but as if everything he had experienced had only been a dream – and then, when she had felt and acknowledged the insignificance of his adventure, he would confess that it had indeed been real. Real? he asked himself – and at that moment became aware of something very close to Albertine's face on the other pillow, on *his* pillow, something dark and quite distinct, like the shadowy outline of a human face. His heart stood still for an instant until he grasped the situation, and, reaching out, he seized the mask he had worn the previous evening, which evidently had slipped out without his noticing that morning as he rolled up his costume, and which the chambermaid or even Albertine herself must then have found. So he could scarcely doubt that after this discovery Albertine must suspect something, and conceivably worse things than had actually happened. Yet the way she had chosen to let him know this, the idea of laying out the dark mask on the pillow next to her, as if to represent his, her husband's face, which had become a riddle to her, this witty, almost light-hearted approach, which seemed to contain both a mild warning and a willingness to forgive, gave Fridolin reason to hope that, remembering her own dream, she would be disposed not to take whatever might have happened all that seriously. But then suddenly, feeling utterly exhausted, Fridolin let the mask slip to the floor and to his own surprise broke into loud, heart-rending sobs, sank down beside the bed and wept quietly into the pillow.

A few seconds later he felt a soft hand stroking his

hair. He raised his head and from the bottom of his heart cried, 'I'll tell you everything.'

At first she gently raised her hand as if to prevent him, but he seized it and held it in his own, both questioning her and pleading with her as he looked up, so she nodded her consent and he began.

By the time Fridolin had ended the first grey light of dawn was coming through the curtains. Albertine had not once interrupted him with curious or impatient questions. She seemed to sense that he had no desire to conceal anything from her, that he was indeed unable to. She lay there quietly, her hands behind her neck, and remained silent a long time after Fridolin had finished. At last – he had been lying stretched out by her side – he bent over her and, gazing into her impassive face and large bright eyes, in which the day now seemed to be dawning too, asked hesitantly yet full of hope, 'What should we do, Albertine?'

She smiled, hesitated briefly, then answered, 'I think we should be grateful to fate that we've emerged safely from these adventures – both from the real ones and from those we dreamed about.'

'Are you quite sure of that?' he asked.

'As sure as I am of my sense that neither the reality of a single night nor even of a person's entire life can be equated with the full truth about his innermost being.'

'And no dream,' he sighed quietly, 'is altogether a dream.'

She took his head in both her hands and pillowed it tenderly against her breast. 'Now we're truly awake,' she said, 'at least for a good while.' He wanted to add: for ever. But before he had a chance to speak, she laid a finger on his lips and whispered as though to herself, 'Never inquire into the future.'

And so they both lay there in silence, both dozing now and then, yet dreamlessly close to one another – until, as every morning at seven, there was a knock upon the bedroom door and, with the usual noises from the street, a triumphant sunbeam coming in between the curtains, and a child's gay laughter from the adjacent room, another day began.

Guy de Maupassant · *Moonlight* · 9780241619803

Carson McCullers · *The Ballad of the Sad Café* · 9780241590546

Yukio Mishima · *Death in Midsummer* · 9780241630853

Vladimir Nabokov · *Nabokov's Dozen* · 9780241630884

Anaïs Nin · *A Spy in the House of Love* · 9780241614686

George Orwell · *Shooting an Elephant* · 9780241630099

Dorothy Parker · *Big Blonde* · 9780241609934

Edgar Allan Poe · *The Masque of the Red Death* · 9780241573754

Alexander Pushkin · *The Queen of Spades* · 9780241573761

Rainer Maria Rilke · *Letters to a Young Poet* · 9780241620038

Françoise Sagan · *Bonjour Tristesse* · 9780241630891

Saki · *Reginald's Christmas Revel* · 9780241597026

Arthur Schnitzler · *Dream Story* · 9780241620229

Sam Selvon · *Calypso in London* · 9780241630877

Georges Simenon · *My Friend Maigret* · 9780241630792

John Steinbeck · *Of Mice and Men* · 9780241620236

Leo Tolstoy · *The Cossacks* · 9780241573778

Yuko Tsushima · *Territory of Light* · 9780241620243

Sylvia Townsend Warner · *Lolly Willowes* · 9780241573785

Edith Wharton · *Summer* · 9780241630815

Oscar Wilde · *The Star-Child* · 9780241597033

Virginia Woolf · *Street Haunting* · 9780241677100

Stefan Zweig · *Chess* · 9780241630822

For rights reasons, not all titles available in the USA and Canada.